**Novel by Neal Barrett, Jr.
based on the screenplay by
Chuck Pfarrer and Adam Rifkin**

B🬀XTREE

First published in the UK in 1996 by Boxtree Limited, Broadwall House, 21 Broadwall, London, SE1 9PL

ISBN: 0 7522 0199 9

10 9 8 7 6 5 4 3 2 1

Typeset in Sabon by SX Composing DTP, Rayleigh, Essex
Printed and bound in Great Britain by
Cox & Wyman, Reading, Berkshire

A CIP catalogue entry for this book is available from the British Library

Check out the Barb Wire Movie Soundtrack on London Records

Triumph Motorcycles, the official bike of Barb Wire

In 1858, President Lincoln said, "A house divided against itself cannot stand." One hundred and fifty years later the house fell.

It was a horror almost impossible to conceive. The United States government was overthrown from within, and the nation was plunged into a second civil war.

The reins of power were seized by a group calling themselves The Congressional Directorate. They suspended the Constitution in the name of new Justice.

And a mighty war began . . .

– Johnny Gray Wolf, Phd, *Fall From Glory* (2032), University of the New Sioux Nation Press.

One

A chill morning fog veiled the foul black waters of the bay. Dark islands rose through the mist, the rusted hulls and twisted stacks of a hundred phantom ships. Once, in the beginning, people had taken shelter in this sunken fleet, hiding from the terrors of the war. No one went there now, not even the new breed of rats the size of dogs. Now the harbor was a deadly chemical soup, the water so thick and turgid a man could breathe its vapors, fall into the dense coagulation, and lie there for a day before the toxic muck began to pull him down.

The biker didn't glance at the harbor, didn't smell the death and decay. The big machine roared through the ghost of the city, past the gutted towers, past the burned-out stores, past the streets filled with misery and pain.

The biker knew the way through the ruined and twisted ways, through the clotted avenues. Still, taking a turn too quickly through the corpses of Toyotas, Oldsmobiles and Cads, the tires hit something wet and dead. The black hog went into a skid; the biker cursed and jerked the handlebars, bulled the monster back in line and thundered off again.

A mother in rags pulled her child out of sight, huddled in the cardboard shelter where they'd spent a fearful night. For a moment the child forgot its empty

1

belly. He stared at the shiny machine, at the driver dressed in fine black leather, at the beetle-dark helmet that hid the biker's face. Where did such a being come from, where did it live? "Hush," the mother said.

Half a block away, a man slid out of his hidey-hole to watch this marvel pass, watched with a hunger, with a longing, with a need that was nothing like the child's.

The biker sped straight through the bowels of the city, through the pall of smoke from a thousand morning fires, sped into the pale diminished sun. On a low flat plain near the far edge of town, the biker paused to study the low brick building and the chain-link fence, the guard shack put together out of spit and rusty tin. The biker made a picture, studied the image, saw it all happen, ran it through again. Then, laughing aloud behind the faceless mask, the biker leaned into the machine, gripped the handlebars and twisted the throttle hard. The engine shrieked, the rear wheels whined and coughed a plume of dust into the air.

The watchman dozed in his shack, slumped in a broken chair. He dreamed of lightning and thunder, of a storm that shook the world, woke to a roar he could feel in his belly and a single searing light.

"Son of a – *bitch*!"

The wind from the black hog whipped him off his feet. He caught a quick flash of the black-clad driver, bent nearly double over the dark machine. The bike hit the gate at sixty-two-point-eight, shattered the lock and sent chain-link twisting in the air.

The watchman picked himself up and scrambled for the walkie-talkie on the floor of the shack. The biker looked back, wrenched the machine in a quick three-sixty, slicked a stubby shotgun from a leather-clad leg. The guard yelled as the radio exploded in his hands. He stared at his fingers, stunned to discover they were all still there.

The big machine's gears shrieked up to a whine, and the hog raced forward, straight for the building fifty yards away. The biker waited, felt the super-charged engine climb to eighty . . . eighty-three . . . eight-five – sucked in a breath, thumbed a red switch on the handlebars . . .

The bike leaped off the ground, the biker fought to bring it down. Twin rockets blasted from either side, wailed like banshees and rushed in drunken arcs towards the solid brick wall. The missiles streaked to their targets, struck an inch apart, blossomed in a yellow fireball, punched out a six-foot hole.

The biker reached through choking smoke and flame. A leather boot slammed against the floor. The bike burned rubber, spun in a donut and jerked to a stop.

Dark machinery squatted in shadow. A maze of pipes hung from the ceiling, squeezed the pumping engines in a tangle of metal vines, thrust through the walls and through the floor. In the heart of the factory a massive generator throbbed with awesome power. The biker drew an object from the black leather jacket, slammed it against the metal wall. The object looked like a bright poison fruit, like a cobalt tennis ball. The biker punched a button in the ball, watched a blood-red LED count ten . . .

nine . . .

eight . . .

seven . . .

3

The biker jerked the hog around and sped for the gutted brick wall. The LED blinked six . . .

five . . .

four . . .

The watchman stared as the biker raced toward him again. The mirrored helmet snapped up, and the biker cried, "Get your ass *outta* here, man!"

The black hog passed in a blur. The watchman turned and ran. The LED blinked three . . .

two . . .

one . . .

The building vanished in a sphere of awful light. Thunder shook the earth; a column of fire and oily smoke licked the morning sky. A wall of heat knocked the watchman to his knees. The action saved his life, as half a ton of superheated steel screamed by above his head . . .

The biker watched from a ruined bridge above the dark waters. The sun was a scabrous orange, draining its venom into another day. Across the river that snaked into the bay, a thin column of smoke rose from the burned-out building. Flames still smoldered on jagged steel debris tossed a hundred yards away. Now and then a bright flare sparked, small electric fires from live cables that sizzled amid the twisted wreckage.

The biker smiled. Even the looters and the goonies wouldn't snoop around that place for a while. Anything you snatched in there would very likely bite back.

A slight, hot breeze stirred the litter on the bridge. The biker shed leather gloves, reached up and

4

removed the black helmet. With a sigh she ran her hands through tawny golden hair, shook her head and let the thick mane tumble past her shoulders. The pale dawning light turned her skin a dusky gold. Startling blue eyes were set wide above proud cheekbones, a regal nose and a mouth that was a little too wide for her face. She sat back on the bike, squinted at the sun and sniffed the morning air. There was the scent of burning wood, the smell of sweat and fear and, underlying all else, the odor of hopelessness and despair.

"My God, you stink," she said aloud, letting her eyes sweep across the city. "Anyplace stinks as bad as you do ought to be dropped in a hole somewhere!"

The city's name was Steel Harbor.

Her name was Barb Wire.

She was the only touch of beauty in the ugliest town in the world . . .

The conquerors moved swiftly. Anarchy reigned supreme. Almost overnight, America changed from a land of plenty to a land where the supermarkets were empty and nothing would grow anymore. People who used to watch third world hunger on public TV could now see it mirrored in their own children's eyes.

Law and order disappeared. The cities burned, and madmen ruled the land. The terrible conflict spread from sea to sea. New York . . . Chicago . . . Houston . . . LA . . . Firestorms raged through the once proud cities, turning every home and building into chambers of the dead.

The cities that didn't die lay under siege of the Congressional armies. Kansas City . . . Phoenix . . . Miami . . . Hunger and thirst finally drove the rebel forces out. Tulsa . . . Seattle . . . Boston fought back.

Every city was at war.

Every city but one . . .

With the aim of bringing some kind of order to the land, the United Nations mandated one city as neutral turf, a cease-fire zone. They picked a good spot . . . a place where there was nothing worth fighting over, nothing left to steal. Everyone who was still alive here was too tough to kill.

The sign on the bridge read:
STEEL HARBOR: DMZ.
And someone had added in a blood-red
scrawl:

THE LITTLE CITY WITH THE GREAT BIG HEART.

– Johnny Gray Wolf, PhD, *Fall From Glory* (2032),
University of the New Sioux Nation Press.

Two

The woman screamed.

It was a ragged, hopeless cry, weakened by unspeakable pain, by the knowledge that no one could help her, that no one could hear.

She hung from her wrists, bound by bright electric cords. Her feet were two inches from the floor. Her head hung limp; her damp hair clung like seaweed to her face. The cotton print dress she had worn when they caught her was now a tattered rag.

Bright silver wires ran from a dozen points on her body, snaking across the floor to a shiny black machine. The woman didn't know about the wires, didn't know about the shiny black machine. She knew the man hurt her, but she didn't know why.

She'd been hanging there for two days now, hanging by the check-out counter of an abandoned auto-parts store. The shelves in the store were empty. Looters had long since stripped the place bare. They had tried to steal the shelves, but the shelves wouldn't go through the door.

There was a time in the country when people had trouble getting parts. Now, in thousands of cities across the land, people had millions of shiny parts – chrome parts, metal parts, parts of every shape and sort. The only things they didn't have were cars.

The man's name was Victor Pryzer. He was a colonel in the Congressional Army, a short and blocky man with a face like raw hamburger and eyes dark as mud. Most colonels wore plain khaki or camou uniforms. Colonel Victor Pryzer had stumbled on a dry goods store while searching for unbroken booze, and he'd designed an outfit of his own. It was gall-bladder black, with gold swirls up and down the jacket, up and down the sleeves and up and down the pants. Swirls on his collar and swirls on his high peaked cap. He had looked really fine until acid in the air turned the gold a bilious green. Now he looked like something from the deep, but no one had the nerve to tell him that.

Pryzer studied the woman a moment, then stepped up and brushed a wisp of hair from her face. The woman gasped, opened her eyes and jerked her head away.

Pryzer shook his head and sighed. "Listen, is it me, or do we have a problem here, what? I think we got a problem here. What I think we got to do is start over from the beginning and try and get it right this time."

The woman desperately tried to work her mouth. "Told you . . . tol' you . . . ever'thing . . . I know . . ."

"Now see that's not working for me," Pryzer said. "This is working for you, it's not working for me. You aren't trying is what it is. What you got to do is *try*."

Pryzer glanced at his watch. This wasn't where he wanted to be. He wanted to be where it was cool and where he couldn't smell sweat and where the walls weren't plastered with pictures of tires.

"I am unhappy with you, Citizen, you are wasting

9

a *lot* of my time. We going to try this time or what? We going to lie, we going to play games, we gonna what?"

"I don't – know," the woman cried, "don't *know*!"

"Yeah, right, you don't know. Me, I think you know."

Pryzer left the woman and walked to her right. The silver wires ran from her body to the shiny black box. On the top of the box was a monitor screen. Vague, distorted pictures swam across the screen. Pryzer held a laser scalpel in his hand and spoke to someone off-screen. The doctor blurred and disappeared ... Pryzer saw a Congressional ID card with the picture obscured ... he saw a giant eyeball, a stark and very clinical view, closer than he really cared to see ... a contact lens slid into sight and the eyeball blinked away ... an empty field, lightning and a dark driving rain ... a man and a woman ... shadows fleeing through the night ...

Pryzer shook his head. His boots were too tight. There was no place clean in this outlandish store to sit down.

"You say no, but your thoughts are up here, your thoughts are saying yes. What am I going to do? You aren't helping, you aren't *sharing* everything with me."

An image flashed on the screen. The woman was dressed in a camou suit. She stabbed Pryzer over and over with an enormous butcher knife. Pryzer fell apart, and blood ran down the screen.

Pryzer smiled. "Well, you're sharing, okay, but it's not exactly what I had in mind."

He stepped over the silver wires and stood at the

black machine. Squinting at the console, he tapped the proper keys. A computer image appeared on the screen, a wire-frame diagram of the human female form. Pryzer picked up a heavy glove and tugged it on his right hand. The glove was made of dull mesh. He looked at the woman again.

"You remember the question, Citizen. Where is she? Where is Dr. Corrina Devonshire?"

The woman wet her lips. A hoarse sound came from her throat. "Don't kn –"

Pryzer's fingers touched the image on the screen. The silver wires shivered. The woman screamed. Her arms and legs spasmed like a puppet gone mad. An angry red welt appeared just above her collarbone. Pryzer smelled the odor of burning flesh.

The woman tried to speak. Pryzer was getting bored, he was getting tired of this. He touched his finger to a point below the abdomen on the screen. The woman shrieked. The sound hurt Pryzer's ears.

Pryzer stopped. He walked back to the woman. Her head slumped on her chest. Pryzer tilted up her chin.

"Look, I got to tell you this, Citizen. I am getting a little pissed. It's no more Mr. Nice Guy, okay? Now talk to me, friend."

The woman's eyes glazed. "She's – sheez . . ." The words bubbled out. ". . . Going to . . . Steel Harbor . . . fruh – free city . . ."

Pryzer let out a breath. "Well now, it's good to share, isn't it? You feel good, I feel good, we don't mess around anymore. Now why is Dr. Devonshire going to Steel Harbor, what's she got to do there?"

He could see it in her eyes, the confusion rising up

11

through the pain. She couldn't really see him, didn't know anymore, didn't know herself, didn't even know her name.

"She –. She's meeting m-members of . . . resish – resishtance . . . they givin' her the . . . retuh – retuh –"

"Retinal," Pryzer helped. "They'll give her the retinal lenses, right?"

The woman almost smiled. "Yes . . . give her the lenses . . . help her get into . . . Canada."

"Canada, is it? Well, now that's fine." Pryzer leaned toward her. He held his breath against the sour smell. "And where are these retinal lenses? Who has them *now*?"

"K-K-Krebs." The words slipped through her dry lips. "Willa – William Krebs . . ."

"And how are they getting into Steel Harbor, how are they planning on that?"

"Wha – whasa?"

The woman's eyes clouded over, went blank. Pryzer slapped her hard. She gasped and tears filled her eyes. He knew she'd come back from the edge, that he'd almost lost her there.

"Had . . . plastic surgery . . . face is changed . . ." The woman's mouth curled in a terrible grin. "You won't . . . recognize her now . . . never find her, you bastard, never f –"

Colonel Pryzer turned to the screen and jabbed his finger right between the image's eyes.

He didn't hear the woman, didn't turn around. He stalked out of the store and lit the stub of a cigar. He made a mental note to find out what fool had brought the woman to an auto parts store. He didn't know a

12

thing about cars, and he didn't like people who did. Before the war he'd sold office supplies. Office supplies were fine, you knew where you were all the time. A pencil was a pencil and you didn't need a goddamn map to figure which end was what.

The officer was standing at the curb, talking to Pryzer's driver. He turned and saw the strange uniform, saw the stubby cigar, saw the storm on the stocky colonel's face. He snapped to attention and stared at a point in outer space.

Pryzer passed him by and ducked through the Caddy's door.

"Executive Council, sir," the driver said. "On the horn, Line 2."

Pryzer didn't hear him. He was staring at the officer now.

"Who are you? What's your name, boy?"

"Hooker, sir. Lieutenant H-Hooker. I'm –"

"You from that jerk-off Counter Intel outfit? Huh? You bring me down here?"

Hooker swallowed hard. "No, sir. I'm with the –"

"Clean up this mess, *Sergeant*. Burn it, hose it down, blow it up. Mac, get me the hell outta here."

Mac slammed the door and ran back to the front. The Caddy burned rubber. Hooker smelled cheap gas. He smelled the cheap cigar. He wondered what to do next. He'd never seen Pryzer before, but he knew who he was and he knew what he did. Whatever was in that building, he knew it was something that he, Lieutenant Jack Hooker, would never want to see.

He thought about PFC DiBello who worked in the motor pool and went through the lines all the time to

13

see his girl. DiBello didn't like lieutenants, but Hooker had looked the other way and never said a thing about the girl. Tonight might be a good time to see DiBello and think about another career . . .

Three

The monitor was built into the seat behind the driver. Someone had screwed it in crooked, and Pryzer wondered who was responsible for that. The army wasn't like business. Things got broken, things didn't work. As long as it wasn't your ass, nobody cared.

The screen flickered, blinked, filled with the image of C. J. 'Jack' Foster. Foster had a face like a horse. He had an Adam's apple the size of Pryzer's nose. He was freshly shaved and he'd cut himself twice. He wore a suit and a tie, and his shirt was a size too large. Pryzer was sure the man was used to farmer's overalls. It amazed and horrified Pryzer that this goofball was actually in a position of power, high enough to screw up the works, high enough to screw up Pryzer himself if he had the sense to know how . . .

FOSTER
Afternoon, Colonel. You got any word yet on our traitorous doctor, Cora D.?

PRYZER
Hey, cut the Cora D. crap. I don't go for that spook talk, mister.

FOSTER
Ah, you're right, of course. Everybody does it up here,

15

you get in the habit. Dr. – Dr. Corrina Devonshire, okay? She's a mighty big problem to the Congressional interests, Colonel. Got to get on her, got to run her down –

PRYZER

[*Leans forward and pokes a big finger at the screen.*] Hey, I don't know that? You think I don't know that?

FOSTER

I'm just saying, I can't stress how essential it is to bring this person back to Washington. Intact.

PRYZER

Good. Then don't.

FOSTER

What's that?

PRYZER

You can't stress. Fine. Then don't.

FOSTER

What I'm meaning to say, Colonel, is Dr. Cora D. – Dr. Devonshire – was privy to some of the most sensitive secrets of the Congressional republic. She's got to be caught at any cost. It behooves you –

PRYZER

[*Slams the screen with his fist. Foster looks startled. His face swims out of shape, then snaps back in place.*] I'll *handle* your problem, *Citizen*. All right? I'll get my hands dirty for you jerkoffs – again.

FOSTER

Colonel Pryzer –

PRYZER

Shut it, pal. I don't want to hear it, I don't want to *talk* to you, I don't want to see your ugly face. I wouldn't *have* to be scrapin' up your mess if you morons hadn't let this woman get away in the first place.

FOSTER

Yes, well . . . I think you have to understand, sir, that we have a number of –

PRYZER

She's as good as caught. I'm not losing this war because a bunch of lame politicians can't hang on to one turncoat bitch!

FOSTER

I'm going to have to ask you to remember who you're talk –
  Click!

The takeover caught the United States at its lowest hour. The government was bankrupt and the economy was struggling to survive. Only the army – secretly supported by Congress – had any strength at all. And, for the most part, the military was a rag-tag shadow of its former self. Only the lack of any real opposition made it a telling force. Corruption stood in for honor and respect. Brutality took the place of strategy and command.

As a result, men came to power who would have blessedly remained in obscurity if there had never been a war.

– Johnny Gray Wolf, PhD, *Fall From Glory* (2032),
University of the New Sioux Nation Press.

Four

The small boat was almost invisible against the skeletal hulls and the dark polluted night. The man called Axel Hood dipped an oar into the muck. It was like rowing through a black sea of molasses, only molasses didn't stink. Every time he stirred the sluggish waters some foul and ancient odor rose to join the already poisoned air of Steel Harbor.

Resting a moment, he glanced at the woman. She sat straight in the bow of the boat, holding a scarf to her face, covering her nose and mouth. She sensed that he was watching, turned to him and lowered the scarf and smiled. He was used to her now, and he knew what she was doing; she was telling him she was fine, that nothing bothered her at all.

Axel knew she wasn't fine. She was struggling to keep her lunch down. She couldn't give in to this very human act because she was Cora D., and a legend didn't throw up like everybody else.

The dim glow of the city reflected off the water and etched her features in yellow light. For a moment Axel was startled by the sight. With her black-agate eyes and the flesh drawn tight about her face, she looked more like a statue than a woman, an ebony goddess, an idol from a city on the Nile. She was tall and lean, soft as a silken pillow and hard as nails.

Axel admired her and respected her courage, but he

wasn't sure he could ever be attracted to a woman like Cora D.. He'd done that one, with disastrous results. Going halfway with a woman was fine; a woman who wasn't strong enough to handle herself wasn't worth the time of day.

So how come I always get tangled with a mean, stubborn, rowdy female – a woman who won't give a bloody inch?

He didn't know the answer. He hadn't know it then, and he damn sure didn't know it now.

On the far shore a car's light winked three times and went out. Axel drew a breath.

"It's them," he whispered. "Keep down, I'm goin' to try and take this garbage scow right under the pier."

"There are rats under there," the woman said. "I can hear them."

"This is Steel Harbor," he told her. "There are rats everywhere."

The woman sat very still and didn't look at him again. Axel had to smile. How about that? The legend of the Resistance didn't care for rats. Maybe she was real after all.

He rowed up under the pier, quietly shipped his oars and reached out to touch the damp piling. The rats were there, all right. He could smell them, see their red eyes in the dark, hear them scuttering over-head. He tried to help her out of the boat. She shrugged him off and climbed the short ladder herself.

The car was a junker – rust and broken glass, held together with duct tape and wire. Two men sat in the front. It was clear they didn't intend to get out.

Axel stepped in front of the woman. He stopped five feet from the car.

"We're looking for Krebs," he said. "Which one of you is him?"

"Neither one," said the driver. "We meet him later." He was a man with a flat-top head and a voice like gravel in a can.

"I'm not real good with later," Axel said. "Later gets me real upset. I like things that happen now."

The driver grinned, showing Axel bad teeth. "How about walking, pal, you like walking okay?"

"Maybe walking makes him upset," the other man said. "He looks like a guy, walking makes him upset."

The driver laughed. "Yeah, he does. That's what he look likes to me."

"Forget it," Cora D. said, "get in."

Axel shrugged. The woman gave him a look and slid past him into the car. Axel got in and the driver took off at once, slamming his passengers hard against the seat.

"Slow down," Axel yelled, "we're not in a big hurry, pal!"

"I'm driving," the driver said. "I'm driving, I don't need any help from you."

"He's driving," the guy beside him said. He was the counterweight to his friend, short and skinny with too much hair. "The man knows how to drive, he don't need any help from you."

"He needs a leash is what he needs."

"Whassat?" The driver turned around in his seat. "What'd you say? You hear him, Jackie, what'd he say?"

21

Cora D. sucked in her breath. "Shut up. All of you. Get me where we're going, you can kill each other for all I care."

"Sounds fine to me," the driver said, "sounds like a – *son of a bitch!*"

A big truck suddenly loomed out of the night, veered into the junker's path and filled the car with searing light. The driver cursed and jammed his foot to the floor. The car turned in a dizzy half circle and jerked to a stop.

"Customs! Out of the car, everybody out!"

"Oh, nice," Axel said.

Two men spilled out of the truck, one from each side. They both held shotguns leveled at the car.

"Stay inside," the driver said, "we'll handle this."

Axel didn't answer. He slid down in the seat, edging toward the door, his hand on the handle. the driver and his passenger walked towards the front of the car.

"This is very bad," Axel said, "this is going south fast. We are in deep do-do here, lady, I hope you can run real fast."

Cora D. gripped the edge of her seat. "I have to get to Krebs. I *cannot* get on the plane without those lenses."

"I'll get you on the plane."

"How? How are you going to do that?" She squinted at the truck. "What are they doing, what's happening out there?"

"I don't know, just take it easy."

"I will not take it easy. Don't you *ever* tell me to take it easy!"

"Okay. Fine. Panic then, lady. See what tha –"

22

The shot was a deep muffled sound, like a big animal coughing in the night. The driver flew back against the hood, slid to the ground. The passenger pulled a gun from his jacket, walked backward and emptied his weapon at the truck. The shotguns roared twice. The man's face disappeared and the windshield spidered with blood.

Axel didn't take time to think. The only really *good* idea he'd had since the whole business started was not to get *in* the junker car and it was too late for that. He muttered under his breath, opened the rear door on the driver's side and kicked it back hard.

The door slammed open. Shotguns blazed, glass shattered and the door ripped off its hinges and clattered into the night. Axel was already out of the far door, holding Cora D.'s wrist and pulling her into cover in the alley to their right. One of the men spotted them and yelled. Gunfire raked the night, ripping our mortar and scaring the rats.

A garbage can exploded, showering the valley with rotten food. Lead whined off the street and stitched the brick walls, and Axel knew at once there was too much firepower here, there were too many guns, there were sure as hell more than two men back there.

They were waiting . . . the bastards knew we were coming, they were already there.

Cora D. shouted something he couldn't hear. Light burned his eyes and a pistol went off three feet from his head. Axel ducked blindly to his right, lashed out with his elbow and struck the man solidly in the throat. He saw the other man look up out of shadow and knew he was a second too late. Cora D. said, "*Huuuh!*" and struck Alex's assailant in the back.

She stared at the brick in her hand and looked surprised. The man staggered back, reached out for the wall. Axel brought his fists together in a club and slammed them against the man's neck.

Cora D. rolled her eyes. "Great. Now what?"

"Now we get the hell out of here and find your friend Krebs."

Cora D. made a noise in her throat. "You don't have any idea where he is. How do you intend to do that?"

Men shouted down the alley. Someone blew out windows with automatic fire.

"You won't like it," Axel said, "don't ask."

Five

"What do you mean she got away?" Pryzer screamed into the phone. "She couldn't get away, she – What are you shooting at, Major? She got away, what the hell are you shooting at down there? Nobody's there, what the hell are you – Rats? You're shooting at rats? I don't want any rats, you goddamn moron. I WANT CORRINA DEVONSHIRE AND I WANT HER RIGHT NOW!"

Six

Short Guy was wearing a holo-plaid jacket in nine shades of red, bicep boosters and built-in pecs, gut-slims and stud-butts, hop-boots and highs, and the Big Guy Cod Number Nine. The face job said twenty, the eyes said fifty-five.

He squeezed his way through, nodding at the hip and spangled guys, like they shared a secret sin. He winked at the cool and nasty ladies, and the ladies cut him down with their razor-blade eyes.

Neon splashed in the rain-wet streets. The sign above the door sizzled HAMMERHEAD BAR & GRILL. Short Guy sighed at the girl with golden legs and blue hair. A biker with a King George wig looked down at him and smiled.

Short Guy didn't care. Nobody knew him, he was out and they were in, he loved them every one, they were all his close friends.

He snaked through the crowd to the front of the line, grinned at the bouncer dressed in shiny blue lamé, a really big dude nearly eight feet high.

"Hey hey, Her-cue-leez, my man. I need to be *inside*. Got to get in, gotta meet with the lovely Barb Wire."

"Right," said the bouncer, "back of the line, pal."

"*Front* works better for me, I don't *do* lines, man." Short Guy winked at the monster, slipped two Cs in his vest. "You dig what I mean?"

The bouncer didn't look down. He lowered the rope and let three more patrons in the bar.

"Hey man!" Short Guy tugged at his sleeve. "You hear what I'm saying, I *laid* some goodie on you."

"I appreciate it, too. Back of the line, *man*."

"Listen here, big guy. There are people I know, you understand? People goin' to –"

The bouncer picked him up gently by the collar, kicked him in the rear and tossed him through the crowd. Short Guy hit the street and bounced. The real hip guys and the cool chicks laughed. Short Guy looked up and grinned. His happy-hair squeaked and scuttled back onto his head.

Short Guy sat there and looked at the lights. The street didn't smell real good, but nobody noticed anymore. Two UN troopers sauntered by. One reached down and helped him to his feet.

"Better get home before you get yourself killed," a soldier said.

"Got things to do, got to get me *inside*." Short Guy brushed himself off, peeled a piece of garbage off his cuff. "Got a date with Barb Wire. Can't be standing here messin' with you."

The first soldier winked at his friend. "Don't bother the man. He's got a date with Barb Wire."

The second trooper grinned. "Don't everybody, man?"

"Hey, soldier dude, don't be fooling with me."

Soldier Dude laughed, picked up Short Guy and walked him back to the crowd.

"Bar-bear-ee-uns, what you are," Short Guy muttered to himself. "Mr. Hired Gun don't scare me."

Short Guy smelled bad breath and whiskey, coke

and sweat and death. He turned around and bumped into a very tall blonde.

He said, "Hey there, darlin', I got the time, the money and the tools to make you feel real fine."

"Raymond's the name, and gasoline's the game," the blonde said. "We gonna burn up your face or mine?"

Seven

The guy's name was Stitch. He was dressed in a pink fishnet and he was scarred from head to toe. If you asked him, he'd tell you he'd been cut and patched eight hundred sixty-two times.

Tina Lou was repulsed. She'd worked at the Hammerhead a year and a half. She could handle most any kind of kink but a Painer made her ill. Why would you let a jerk hurt you real bad when you could be hurting *him* It didn't make a lot of sense.

Stitch tried to wander by, tried to sneak through the lobby to the inside door.

"Just hold it," Tina Lou said, "you been here before. Check your weapon, man."

Stitch looked contrite. He laid an ugly hunk of metal on the counter, a gun so rusted, so pitted and slagged, she knew he must have made it himself.

"Nice piece," she said, flipping him a token. "Fifty Cal Plus?"

"Sixty-two," Stitch said. "Double-fire, semi-modified. Acid balls or a triple load of red."

"Sounds groovy, man."

Stitch tried to smile, an awful thing to see. He opened the door and walked in. The noise from the Hammerhead hit him with thirty-two Gs. The band was Open Wound, and the sound was a nasty mix of rap and rip and rock, death-cry and doom.

Stitch breathed in the sound, felt the music in his skin, in his organs, in his bones. He heard something snap, heard something crack and tear. Looked down and saw he was bleeding from a hole above his heart.

"All right," he said, shaking to the sound, "we are havin' fun now!"

The decor of the Hammerhead was white table-cloths, rubble and Cadillac chrome. Satin and silk, camou and fear. A mix of Late Napalm and Pre-War Glitz.

Curly made his way through the crowd with a waiter's practiced skill. He'd worked there too long and he didn't hear the laughter, didn't hear the din.

Two shady dealers hunched across a table in the rear. One wore a mohawk, one wore a blue electric suit. Curly left their gin, let them know he didn't see their smack, didn't see the sack of cash.

Giggles from the Number One booth to Curly's right. The four chickies twined like pretty little snakes around the oldest man in town.

"Dry martini, three olives, sir, and your Cuban cigars," Curly said.

"Atta boy, son." The old man flipped him a C. "Ask Barb to join us for a drink when she can."

"You got it, Senator."

Curly moved along. The Congressional troopers had a table of their own and an endless supply of bawdy songs. Not far away, the American soldiers tried to drown them out. Half a dozen UN warriors sat at the bar and scowled at their drinks. Curly didn't care for that. Quiet soldiers made him uneasy. Somehow it didn't seem right.

He headed for the stairs, saw the apparition coming at him, an overweight sheik in a robe like a runaway tent. He tried to get away, but the Arab cut him off.

"Curly, my good friend, I am yet waiting to hear from the desirable and wondrous Miss Wire. I have been most patient, yes?"

"She got your message," Curly said. "Fifteen hundred Cs, she chops off your brother's legs. Barb says no, she doesn't do that kind of work. Says you ought to be ashamed of yourself."

The sheik looked alarmed. "She says this? I cannot believe you. Waiters are the sons of swine, their tongues can speak nothing but lies. No offense, my friend."

"Sure. None taken."

The sheik pushed Curly aside and started up the stairs. "I know what she wants. She is a woman. She desires my affection. She does not wish to speak of money until her needs are satisfied."

"Have at it, Effendi," Curly said.

The sheik took three steps up the stairs. The Rottweiler padded down the landing, looked at the Arab with bloody eyes and growled.

The sheik backed off. Curly leaned down to pet the dog.

"This here's Camille," he said, "Barb's private secretary. You aren't in Camille's appointment book, you're liable to lose your ass."

The sheik swelled up like a toad, started to speak but the words got lost somewhere. Curly watched him stomp away, then started up the stairs. A fight broke out behind him, but he didn't turn around.

Someone else would handle that. Fights weren't his affair.

Open Wound took a break, and the Gut-Shot Five sat in. The music was the same and nobody blinked an eye.

Charlie Kopetski liked the tall ones. He liked them even more if they were slim and had fiery red hair. Even if he couldn't see them anymore, he liked to think about them tall, he liked to think about their hair.

"What I'm thinking," Charlie said, "I'm thinking, this lady's not wearing some wartime shit, this lady's got her some Chanel No. 5. Am I right, am I correct in that?"

The woman looked at Charlie, looked at the fifth double bourbon in his hand, looked at the wrap-around glasses that covered his empty eyes. He'd asked her right off if she was tall and if she had red hair. Neither guess was right, but he was laying down cash and she hadn't tasted vodka in a while.

"Yes," she said, "you are. Now how'd you know that?"

"The Mercedes of perfume, darlin'. A man of dis-crimination knows. I became aware of you, of this . . . scent of queens you wear, and I said to myself, I said, Charles, my man, this is obviously a woman of signipi – significant breeding."

"What a nice thing to say."

"Not at all, merely a reflection of the truth, as any-one can see. Except me, of course, and I can't see shit, you may – maybe noticed that. I said to myself, if she's a lady of blee – breeding, maybe she'd like to . . .

32

engage in a little breeding tonight, yes? Could be, I said, and then when I knew you were of such maf – such magnificent height, I . . ."

"Charlie, who you talkin' to, man?" The bartender leaned in close so he could hear. "I got bad news. The chick is gone, the lady has fled, pal."

"Oh, well . . ." Charlie showed him a crooked smile. "Perhaps she had an apot – apot – appointment of some kind. In that case, I shall have another of these, Fred."

"I can't do it, Charlie. Your sister'll have my ass I let you go fallin' all over the place. She'll –"

Charlie stood abruptly, knocking his barstool to the floor. He clutched his drink in his hand and threw it at the bar. Fred ducked. The glass shattered the mirror and broke five bottles of bathtub scotch.

Charlie stumbled off, flailing his arms and knocking customers aside. Fred made a quick motion across the room. A man built like an oil drum moved through the crowd and gently guided Charlie away.

Barb sat half in shadow behind her desk. On the other side of the room there was a table and a lamp and a straight-back chair. No coffee tables, no magazines. No pictures on the wall. Clutter was for the Hammerhead Bar, clutter sold well down there. In her own hidey-hole Barb liked it simple, plain and neat.

The room was sound-proof, but she could feel the action through the floor. She could look through the one-way window and see the silent chaos down below.

"If this is a good time to talk about the payroll," Curly said, "I'd like to maybe –"

"It's not," Barb said. "What's the traffic like? Looks a little light."

"A little, maybe. Normal Thursday night. Bottom-feeders, high-rollers, every kind of jerkoff in between. Bunch of troopers lettin' off steam."

Barb touched her tongue to her lips. "Tell Tina Lou to double-check those mothers, okay? I don't want any more grenades in here. I like the place just fine the way it is."

"You got it," Curly said. He reached into his apron and tossed a wad of notes on Barb's desk.

"Tonight's fan mail. Three offers to sell black-market dollars. Another offer to buy the bar. A desperate request to contact the Resistance, I don't know who from. A couple of proposals of marriage from a general and a porno king."

Barb didn't even glance at the mail. Curly watched her as she stood and moved restlessly about the room. She was dressed in soft blue leather that clung to her slender body like a kiss. Her corn-silk hair hung loose down to her waist.

Curly had known Barb Wire about as long as anyone else. He saw her every day, brushed up against her and breathed in her animal scent. Such close association had taught him to keep his eyes in neutral and his thoughts to himself.

"I don't like to keep bringing it up, boss, but tomorrow's payday around here. What am I supposed to use for money, you want to tell me that?"

Barb rolled her eyes. "Relax, Curly. I'll come up with it."

"How? Just how do you –"

Curly stopped. Barb moved swiftly across the

34

room, pulled a long duster off a hook and tossed it over her shoulders.

"What, where are we going?" Curly said. "We're going *out*? That's what it looks like to me, it looks like out."

"For a while. That okay with you?"

"Hey, what do I know?" Curly stood and spread his hands. "Don't anyone give me a couple of minutes' notice or anything, don't anyone bother with that. I mean, I love surprises, right?"

Barb grinned. "Stop your bitching, pal. Let's go."

She stepped up to the wall and touched a tiny switch. Something hissed somewhere and a panel slid back. Assault rifles, machine pistols and combat shotguns were neatly racked in the narrow compartment, along with a generous selection of more exotic items: phosphor grenades, stick-ums, whistlers, gutters and a Screaming Freako with a cobalt fuse, a weapon that was outlawed everywhere but Hell.

Barb chose a favourite, a stubby black monster ugly as a hog, checked the magazine, dropped it in a shoulder holster in her cloak.

Curly followed her down the back stairs and into her quarters well apart from the Hammerhead. He tried not to look at the four-poster bed with the red satin sheets, the sunken marble tub. Thoughts like that made him itch all over, and he didn't need that.

Barb's gleaming black and silver bike stood against the bedroom wall. Anyone else, Curly thought, a bike in the bedroom was downright weird. With Barb, it looked just fine.

She rolled the bike down a narrow rampway and into the garage, swung a slim leg across the saddle and kicked the big machine into life. A deep and throaty roar shook the night.

Curly looked at her and frowned. "Listen, Barb, you went out *last* night, it isn't real friendly out there –"

Barb cut him off with a slice of her hand through the air. "That incident never happened. *This* isn't happening either, okay? Anyone asks, I'm taking a bubble bath."

Curly swept that picture out of his head. "I just don't think it's a good idea to –"

"Stop whining. You're the one who said it. We're running short of cash. I'll be back before the second set."

Curly started to speak, but Barb revved up the machine to an ear-splitting roar.

"And keep Charlie out from under the tables," she shouted over the noise. "It's real embarrassing, Curly, my brother's always crawling on the floor."

Barb hit a remote, the door slid open and she disappeared into the dark.

Curly watched until he couldn't hear her anymore. He knew he'd spill a drink tonight, maybe three or four. He took a great pride in his work, and he didn't like that, but he knew he wouldn't think straight until she got back.

The Second American Civil War was known by many names, depending on the source. The Congressional Forces called it 'The Great War of American Freedom', and 'The Patriot's War'. The Resistance called it 'The Tyrant's War', and 'The War of Oppression'.

The great masses, the people of the United States caught up in famine and hardship even before the war began, simply called it Hell. For them there were no catch phrases, no slogans or songs. They didn't know who was winning and didn't care. They already knew who the losers would be . . .

– Johnny Gray Wolf, PhD, *Fall From Glory* (2032), University of the New Sioux Nation Press.

Eight

Barb slowed the big machine, flicked off the lights and coasted down the alley of a burned-out avenue. She waited there and listened, taking in the sounds of the night. A battle-jet far off to the east, past Steel Harbor out in the killing zone. Closer, scattered gunfire. Barb's practiced ear told her it was strictly gang war, yap-dog .25s. Some kid would get a bullet in the belly and the shooter would lose a hand.

The other sound brought her up straight. Nothing much scared her anymore, but the thing she heard now sent a shiver up her spine. Slipping a penlight out of her saddlebag, she swept the narrow alley left and right.

The light caught them cold. Gaunt, white faces and ball-bearing eyes. They blinked at her and scuttled out of sight. Snakers. Cast-offs from both of the armies, men who'd been chewed up so badly they were no good for fighting anymore. They'd all lost their legs, and most of them had lost an arm or two. Now they bellied through the dark of the cities, preying on each other or anything that stopped or slowed down. They were modern-day lepers; no one talked about them, but everyone knew they were there.

In the wars of the century before, Barb knew, men like these could get help. Therapy and artificial limbs would let most of them walk again. That was in the

38

Good Times, though – there was no time now for such nonsense as that.

Barb took a wad of bills from her bag, shined the light in the dark again and tossed the pack across the alleyway. She doused the lights and waited, heard something whisper, heard something scuttle and slide.

A switch on the handlebar brought the holo screen alive in mid-air. Barb punched the keyboard on the dash, and the names flicked by in a blur of green and red. Mary McGore had nothing she cared to see. Same with Tapper Man. A couple of credit jumpers, three or four deserters and assorted minor scum. Barb sighed and punched in again:

THOMAS SCHMITZ
BAIL BONDS
"SERVICE DAY OR NIGHT"

She flipped down the list:

BARROWS, H.R.	*5,000*
CAMERON, J.L.	*5,000*
DEGAS, R.T.	*2,500*
KREBS, W.R.	*10,000*

The fourth name caught her eye. She asked for more details. Unarmed. Not considered dangerous. KREBS, W. R., had jumped bail the week before. The list never told you what they'd done; that was against the law, a breach of civil rights.

What interested Barb was the paycheck, a fat 10K. Ten would get Curly off her back and pay some bills.

Last known address was listed for all offenders, but that was a laugh. None of these sleazeballs were sitting home watching TV, waiting for someone to bring them in.

Barb heard the Snakers again, closer this time. *Hey, if someone was throwing cash around, maybe they had a little more.* Ungrateful bastards. Just try to help someone . . .

She drove the bike three blocks and stopped again, this time in the shell of a bombed-out deli. There was still a glass display case intact and a plateful of petrified gunk.

The screen went black, crackled with snow, then turned blood-red. The voice said:

"This is a recording. Don't call back 'cause nobody's home. This is a recording. Don't call –"

"Owl, it's me," Barb said, "get on the dam screen."

Someone cackled somewhere. The screen turned white and the Owl blinked at Barb. Beer-bottle glasses, unshaven cheeks and a drinker's red nose. A green plastic eyeshade tied around a shiny round dome.

"Hey, Barb, my love. Long time." The Owl showed her a toothy grin. "What you need, hon?"

"Krebs, W. R. Bail-jumper listed with Schmitz. What you got on him?"

Owl's smiled faded. No more social grace, this was business now. He looked away, punched his own keyboard out of sight.

"Krebs, W. R.," he said, glancing back at Barb. "Semi-shady past. Streetwinder, varied cons and scams. Friends and known associates . . . forget it, that's first-level stuff, the cops'll have all that.

40

"Okay, here we go, Barb: Tenebaum, Reuben B.: High-rise, Four-Niner-Seven South 85th. Guy's a real sleazeball. Runs a porno store, street level, two doors down from his own address. He and Krebs pulled a couple of deals together, but the law doesn't know about that. I'd give it a try."

"Thanks," Barb said. "Who else have you sold this to, Owl?"

The Owl looked hurt. "I'm a legitimate business-man, love. I got principles, you know?"

"Right. Who else?"

"No one but you. That doesn't mean someone else doesn't have this stuff beside me. I'm good but so is the Flusher and Mama Greaves."

"How much?"

"Five hundred okay?"

"Three-fifty, Owl. Four if I get a guarantee."

"Get real, Barb. Three seventy-five."

"You got it," Barb said.

The holo disappeared. Barb kicked the hog into action and thundered down the avenue, back the way she'd come. The Snakers watched her pass, saw her lean and slender form, saw her hair whip the breeze, prayed the bike would hit a hole. Prayed it wouldn't hurt the pretty very bad . . .

It was late before he turned off the light, pulled the shades and locked the door. He was a heavy man with no neck and tiny eyes. The brown suit was shiny, a size too tight. Barb thought he looked like a roach.

She timed it so they'd meet before he got very far from his store. He saw her and stopped, and she gave him a dirty smile.

41

"Hi there, handsome. You want some company, love?"

My God, I can't believe I said that . . .

The man's BB eyes gleamed. This vision had to be lost or on smoke. The whores in his neighbourhood *never* looked like this.

"You a cop or what? I don't want any trouble with a cop."

Barb opened her duster wide. "See a badge anywhere?"

The man's jaw dropped. He licked his lips and looked cautiously down the street.

"You got your Med-Reg?"

"Sure do, sweets. Checked out yesterday."

The man studied her card. It read: LICENSE OF PROSTITUTION. There was a small nude holo on the card. He looked at the card a long time.

"How much?"

"Depends on how you want to play."

"I like to . . . I like to play rough."

Barb laughed. "Hey, me too. How 'bout that?"

She looked in his eyes, saw what was there. If he didn't have a stroke in the next two minutes everything would work out fine.

Sandbags and steel mesh blocked the doorway of the high-rise from the street. Barb stood back as the man stuck his card in the slot. A screen came to life. A giant, bloodshot eye appeared in a cross-hair grid.

"Retinal scan verified . . . Thank you, Reuben Tenebaum."

"One guest," Reuben said.

"Accepted."

42

The door hissed open and the doorman stepped back. He lowered his 12-gauge and let the couple by. The lobby was a wreck. An old lady hacked in a battered easy chair. Two characters in suits worse than Reuben's stared at Barb with hungry eyes.

The hall smelled bad. The high-rise wasn't cheap, but in Steel Harbor the rats were everywhere.

Reuben was breathing hard when they reached the fourth floor. He turned the key in Four-Two-Two. It smelled a lot worse inside. it smelled like Reuben Tenebaum. Sweat and sour clothes, take-out food. Videos and porno magazines were stacked along the walls. Barb wasn't surprised. Flesh was Reuben's business, and his full-time hobby, too.

Reuben didn't waste any time. He peeled off his jacket, tossed it toward a chair and grabbed at Barb's breast.

Barb gently fended him off. "I've got a better idea," she said. "Why don't you slip into something a little more comfortable, love."

Reuben gave her a sly grin. "How about something a – a little *un*comfortable?"

"I can hardly wait." She gave him a playful pat. "You hurry now."

She watched him scurry into the bathroom. As the door clicked shut she quickly slid a lipstick case from her bag, plugged in an earpiece and ran the small device over Reuben's east wall. A holo showed bright thermal patterns, vivid reds and yellows, shimmering greens and blues. It was Reuben's bedroom. Nothing. The room to the north was full of porno books.

South wall. There . . . Barb let out a breath. Reuben wasn't as dumb as he looked. His buddy Krebs wasn't in Reuben's apartment – Reuben also had the one next door.

Krebs was asleep. Sprawled on the bed. Barb tossed the device back in her bag. She checked the bathroom door, brought a tiny aerosol and sprayed a wide patch of foam on the wall. The foam hissed, turned rock-hard in the air. Barb punched a detonator tube into the mess, turned and looked around the room. Reuben had a day bed in the corner. She lifted off the mattress and leaned it against the wall. Fine. If the sleazeball would just stay in the bathroom a while . . .

The sleazeball didn't. He opened the door and walked out. He was wearing a tight rubber suit. He blinked at Barb, then grinned at the mattress propped against the wall.

"Wha – what are we going to do now? This is a new one on me."

"We're going to get *down*, hon," Barb said. She grabbed him by the shoulders, pulled him behind the sofa and shoved him to the floor. She raised up, aimed her pistol, and fired at the mattress on the wall.

The wall shook. Plaster cracked and rained down from above. The mattress vanished, and a ragged hole appeared in the wall. Feathers filled the room. Reuben screamed and covered his ears. Barb sprang over the sofa and raced through the hole. Krebs sat up and stared.

"What the bloody *hell* –"

Barb chopped him once across the jaw. Krebs sighed and went limp. Barb jerked handcuffs out of her bag, snapped them on his wrists, lifted his feet and dragged him toward the hole to Reuben's room.

"Why is it every one of you bastards jump bail

44

weights two-eighty-five?" she muttered to herself. "I shoulda brought a tow truck –"

She heard the sound, heard the feet pounding in the hall. She dropped Krebs and rolled as the door exploded off its hinges and flew across the room.

It happened in a blur. Barb knew she was in trouble, knew the intruders were the two from the lobby, knew the guys were pros, that they'd come for Krebs, too.

The first one was big – he came in low, bending at the knees and spraying the room with automatic fire. Barb twisted her hips, kicked a coffee table and sent it sliding across the room. The table hit the shooter in the shins. He howled, dropped his gun and went down.

His buddy came in high. He was short and had a tattooed face. He spotted Barb and let loose with a pump shotgun. A chair shattered against the wall, the TV exploded in a burst of white light. Barb scrambled to her feet and dived through the hole to Reuben's room. Reuben was still screaming, writhing on the floor.

Barb paused an instant, then ran for the kitchen, ducked inside as the scattergun blew Reuben's porno collection all to hell. Flesh-colored confetti fluttered about the living room. Tattoo-face roared, searching for Barb.

Barb peeked from behind the refrigerator. "Hey, over here, stupid!"

Tattoo-face grinned, jacked a shell in the chamber and came at her on the run. Barb swung the refrigerator door in his face. Tattoo met it head on. He stepped back, wobbled and shook his head. Barb shot him through the open door, shot him through two dozen eggs, pickles and a jar of mayonnaise.

She didn't see the big guy – sensed he was there, backed off fast and knew she was a second too late. Her hand went numb. The slug jerked the weapon from her grip, sent it flying out of sight. The shooter came at her through the hole, stitching the air with lead, ripping chunks of plaster from the wall.

Barb went down on her hands and knees, crawled past the kitchen counter toward the living room. A microwave burst into a thousand pieces, showering glass down on her head. She cursed and dived under a table, glanced over her shoulders, came to her feet and faced through a narrow hall.

The shooter stitched the floor in her path. Barb ran, came up flat against a wall. She sucked in a breath. Dead end – the hallway went nowhere at all!

The shooter appeared, the ugly weapon held straight out in his hands. A nasty grin crossed his face.

"Barb Wire herself. Man, wait'll they hear about this!"

He jammed the weapon in Barb's face. Squeezed the trigger. Squeezed it again. His smile disappeared.

"Hey, some days are like that," Barb said. She pressed both hands against the hallway walls, kicked out with both feet and slammed him in the teeth.

The shooter screamed, stumbled back and fell. Picked himself up, saw the ragged hole behind him and retreated to Krebs' room. Barb came at him, lashed out with the stiff edge of her hand, followed with a punishing kick to the jaw.

The big man folded like a sack. Barb turned and lifted Krebs' limp form by the shoulders. The shooter came up on his knees, spat out a tooth and grinned.

"Man, that was nice kickin'. You really know your stuff, babe."

Barb dropped Krebs and stared. "What – *what* did you call me?"

The shooter came to his feet. "Don't get all shook up, okay? I just –"

Barb saw it, then, the flash of a blade coming up fast from his side. She turned, spun on one foot, and buried her boot in his gut.

The shooter opened his mouth and gasped for air, stumbled and flailed his arms. He saw the open window, knew he couldn't stop, grabbed for the curtain, and disappeared.

Barb heard him scream, heard the sound cut short. She went to the window, leaned out and looked down. He was hanging there, the curtain wound tight about his neck. His left hand jerked. His right leg kicked out twice.

Barb shook her head. "Don't call me babe, man. I really *hate* that . . ."

Nine

Thomas Schmitz was a donut with a head on top. The furrows in his doughy face were black with grease. A trail of powdered sugar drifted down his chest to the awesome belly below. The debris stopped there. There was no way to pass this obstacle, nowhere to go.

Schmitz looked up from his oversized chair as Barb Wire kicked in the door, stomped in and dropped Krebs at his feet.

"Well, Mr. Krebs." Schmitz allowed himself a lazy grin. "A pleasure, sir. We've been very concerned about you."

He blinked at Barb, looked her up and down. "And *always* a pleasure to see you, Barb. You're looking quite . . . buoyant and lovely today."

"Can it," Barb said. "You got this jerkoff on your list. Ten grand. That won't cut it this time. Twenty sounds better to me."

Schmitz spread his pudgy hands. "I am a reputable bail bondsman, my dear. You know I don't . . . bargain in these matters. It is ten, as stated. No more."

Barb's eyes flashed. "This mother was armed, dangerous and ugly to boot. Besides, there was a *party* at his place, and some real noisy guests showed up."

Schmitz shrugged. "Now how could I anticipate

that? Bounty hunting is a risky and . . . unpredictable business. You, of all people, should know that."

"Twenty," Barb said. "Twenty, or I throw this one back."

Schmitz looked appalled. "This is extortion, Miss Wire. Outright extortion!"

Barb tossed back her hair and laughed. "Rhino Schmitz is going to talk to *me* about extortion? Get real, friend."

The big man nearly came out of his chair, thought about the effort, and eased himself down. "I do not care for that – that epithet, Miss Wire, and I will not give in to your ridiculous demands."

Barb knew he'd pressed a button somewhere, or the goons were standing by. They stepped from behind a dirty curtain, three gorillas with sawed-off bats.

"Oh, now this is real impolite," Barb said. "I'm ashamed of you, Schmitz."

"Yes, of course." Schmitz scratched at his three-day beard. "I am an officer of the court, Barb. You may consider this an official protest."

"Uh-huh." Barb whipped a pistol from her duster and jammed the muzzle against Krebs' head.

"And *you* can consider this dude dead. Toxic waste, pal."

Barb cocked her pistol. The noise sounded deadly in the small and stuffy room. Krebs' eyes went wide.

A single bead of sweat made its way down Schmitz's flabby cheek.

"I would – be willing to go to fifteen thousand, I believe . . ."

"And I'd be willing to splatter this sucker's brains all over your desk."

Schmitz let out a breath, reached into one of his vast pockets and pulled out a filthy wad of cash.

"No way." Barb shook her head. "Twenty thousand *Canadian*. Stop messing with me, Rhino."

Schmitz winced. "Please. *Don't* call me that." He fumbled around and found another stack. This time the color was blue.

Barb swept up the cash and tossed it in her bag. She let Krebs go. His eyes rolled back and he passed out on the floor.

Schmitz mopped his face with a large bandanna. "As ever, it's been a pleasure doing business, Miss Wire."

Barb smiled and backed toward the door. "If it was a pleasure, *Rhino*, I'd charge a lot more . . ."

It is said that war brings out the best and worst in men. Undaunting displays of courage, bravery and sacrifice are equalled only by acts of brutality, torture and unimaginable horror.

Throughout history, men have ceased to savage one another on special occasions and on certain fields of truce. Soldiers will drink to their foes, toast one another and wish each other well, before returning to the killing fields again. A being from another world might view this sight and wonder: "How do these creatures know when their hatred ends, and when it begins again?"

– Johnny Gray Wolf, PhD, *Fall From Glory* (2032), University of the New Sioux Nation Press.

Ten

The Hammerhead was jumping.

Loonies and Smackers jammed the lobby, drinkers packed the bar. Organ Transplant was hard into a heavy second set. The crowd was mesmerized. Dancers kissed and touched, petted and caressed, writhed and rubbed and vanished and never met again.

Barb never walked down the stairs, Barb flowed . . . Barb moved with a sweet undulation, with a shiver and a sigh, like there might be tiny motors in her hips and in her thighs . . . Golden hair tumbled past her shoulders, brushed her flawless skin . . . breasts swelled rich and creamy under satin red as sin. Black boots hugged her slender legs up to her knees . . . hugged her to her thighs, to a fishnet tease . . . And, as she came down the stairs, every man there had a Barb Wire vision in his head . . . Some were sweet and fine, some were snuggle good . . . and some were as dark and cold as razor dreams . . .

Barb blew a dozen kisses, shook a dozen hands, made her way to Curly's *maitre d'* station across the room.

Curly looked up, relieved, once more, to see her back in one piece. "Everything okay?"

"Candy from a baby," Barb said. She slapped a fat

roll of bills into his hand. "Pay the help, for God's sake."

She caught the worry in his eyes and added, "Take it easy, will you? I'm fine."

"This time, sure," Curly said.

"*Every* time. And don't you forget it, friend."

Barb touched him on the cheek and turned away. The soldier was standing in her path, looking young and big-eared, looking awkward, looking dumb. An army barber had shaved his head in two seconds flat.

"'Scuse me, Miss Wire . . . I'm a – I'm a long way from home, you know? I got to go back up to the front tomorrow. I was – I was wonderin' if you'd – if you'd d-d-d –"

"If I'd dance with you, right?" Barb smiled. "You bet, soldier, what's your name?"

Barb curled one arm around his neck. The soldier's ear turned red.

"Hank. Least I think it is." He showed Barb a goofy grin. "This close to you, Miss Wire, I'm n-not sure."

Barb gave him a twirl or two. He wore the cheap, dyed-blue twill of the American army. On his shoulder was the red infantry tab. The uniformed smelled fresh and new.

And when they bring you back in a sack, what will you look like then?

Barb swept the thought from her mind. The soldier's buddies hooted and howled and stomped their feet.

"Where you from, Hank?"

"Steamboat Springs. That's in Colorado. Or what's left of it, I guess. D-did you hear, Miss Wire? The

Congressionals just occupied Denver. They don't even know if . . . anything's left."

Barb turned away. "I can't keep up," she said quickly. "I don't hear anything, friend."

The soldier gave her a curious look. He started to speak, looked over Barb's shoulder and stared.

The door to the lobby burst open. The big bouncer shook his fists and retreated into the room. A cop in black leather poked the ugly snout of his weapon in the bouncer's big belly. The man growled, showed his teeth and stomped off.

Half a dozen officers poured in past the first, took up a stance and waved their weapons about the room. A tall man, thin as a spider, stepped through the black-clad men. His uniform was gray, his eyes were hidden under bright mirror shades. Someone, in the past, had broken his jaw and left his face out of whack. Barb Wire knew who that was and certainly wouldn't tell.

The tall man fired his pistol in the air. The band stopped, the dancers froze.

"All right, nobody move! Everyone stay where you are!"

"Hey, we don't *need* any heat in here, man!"

"*You*!" The cop in gray poked a finger at the man who'd spoken out. Two officers stepped up and grabbed him, another jammed a black box against his race.

"*Retinal scan is ver-if-ied*" a tinny voice said. "*Law-rence Crab-tree. Five-Seven-Two-three-Niner . . .*"

"Crabtree, huh?" The tall cop scowled at the man's ID. "Your card says Ben Jones, Citizen. Arrest this violator! Next!"

The two cops grabbed another patron. The man whined in protest. A black-clad officer grinned and folded him with the butt of his gun.

Barb cursed under her breath, words that turned the young soldier's face a bright crimson again. She left him, stalked quickly up to the tall guy and thrust her chin in his face.

"Okay, Willis, what the hell's going on? What do you want here?"

Willis grinned, showing horse-sized teeth. "Ah, Barb, lovely to see you again. I –"

"Can it, pal. What gives?"

Willis shook his head and tried to look grave. "Some real messy business tonight, Miss Wire. Double homicide down in the old harbor district."

"So? What else is new?"

"Just doing my job, checking IDs. Trying to keep the peace in this troubled city of ours . . ."

Willis leaned in close enough to give Barb a sample of whiskey breath. "We have, ah . . . reason to believe this crime may be related to . . . certain activities among the Resistance. And – no offense intended, Barb – but the Hammerhead is openly patronized by some of the more . . . nefarious people in town."

Barb folded her arms. "Okay, fine, Willis. So how long do you intend to hassle my customers?"

Willis sighed. "Everything's negotiable, Barb."

"Right. I figured it was. Let's go up to my office. People see me talking to a cop, I'll get a bad reputation."

Willis smiled and followed her across the room. It was always a pleasure to follow Barb Wire anywhere, especially up the stairs.

Helping himself to a cognac, Willis eased himself into a chair and plopped his feet on Barb's desk.

"The place is looking fine, Barb. New bar, great sound system. Sounds real expensive."

"I saved my lunch money," Barb said. "A penny here, a penny there."

"Right." Willis studied the amber liquid, then toasted her with his glass. "A little gun-running here, a bail-jumper there. The occasional . . . midnight devastation."

"I don't moonlight."

"Oh, *I* do. It's very profitable, too."

Barb was getting restless. She'd heard all this before. Willis frequently dropped by for a little extortion and a peek down her dress. Everybody knew the city's chief of police was the biggest crook around. No mean accomplishment in a place like Steel Harbor. Still, this visit didn't *feel* routine, and, above all else, Barb Wire hated surprises.

"So what's with the bullshit arrests? My God, Willis, you sold half of those fake Congressional ID cards yourself. You undercutting your own rackets now?"

"Me?" Willis looked appalled. He stood and walked over to Barb where she sat in a straight-back chair. "The whole floor of a high-rise is blown to shit. Two innocent men are dead. A third, some sleazeball who lived in the place, has taken off for parts unknown. I'm just doing my job, Barb. The citizens of Steel Harbor like to see their chief on top of these things."

Barb looked at the ceiling. "You said the Resistance. What makes you think they're involved?"

"Why do you ask? You know something I don't know?"

"Who would know *anything* you don't, Willis? I can't even imgaine some –"

Willis let his hand slide across her bare shoulder, bent to kiss the back of her neck. Barb pulled away.

"Damn it, that's sexual harassment. What the hell's the matter with you?"

Willis's smile faded. He grabbed her roughly and pinned her against the wall.

"Listen, Barbara *Kopetski*, you can hand me the smart talk some other time, I've got important business to attend to now. I want an answer, and don't screw around. Where is William Krebs? By God, if you tell me you don't know . . ."

"I don't know. Never heard of him."

Willis let out a breath. "I mean it, Barb. The two men who died in that shootout were *my* men. Cops. I had 'em watching this Krebs. They're dead and he's gone. So somebody's a cop killer now."

Barb stood, walked to her desk, leaned against the edge and faced Willis. "And because you don't know where to find this guy, I'm supposed to know?" She tried to read the man, but his eyes were hidden behind the mirror shades. All she could see there was a distorted image of herself.

"Anyway, what's the big deal with this – Krebs character? Why'd do you have your men watching him?"

Willis shook his head. He gazed through Barb's window at the Hammerhead down below. "That's classified police business. I can't discuss that."

"Uh-huh. Well, if you want to find Krebs, maybe

you ought to spend your time looking and less time tryin' to get in my pants."

Willis gave her a nasty grin. He didn't have to say a thing.

"If someone . . . happened to know where this person is, I could make it worth their while."

Barb rolled her eyes. "Goodbye, Willis. Go play with yourself."

He drained his glass and set it on Barb's desk. "By the way, we're expecting some distinguished visitors tomorrow. A Congressional delegation from DC, including First Directorate, Colonel Victor Pryzer. Very important man, Colonel Pryzer. I thought he might be amused by the Hammerhead."

"Anybody's welcome to spend money in here," Barb said. "Even someone from DC."

"What a charming thing to say." Willis stopped at the door. "I don't have to make any more arrests in here. I'd say, the usual . . . three thousand."

"I'd say fifteen hundred. I'm still broke from blowing all my lunch money on that sound system you like so much, and tomorrow's payday to boot."

"Fifteen hundred." Willis frowned. "I *might* have to check some more IDs. Twenty-five."

"Deal."

She reached in her desk and tossed a wad of bills at the chief. Willis scooped it up and shoved it in his jacket.

"It's nice we could get together, Barb."

"No, it's not. And that's three bucks for the cognac."

"Add it to my tab, Miss Kopetski."

She gave him a look Willis felt between his eyes.

58

"Barbara Kopetski died in the war. I'm Barb Wire. Try and remember that, mister . . ."

Eleven

There were moments sometimes, in the hours before the dawn, when the wind picked up and the gray veil of pollution parted to reveal a clear and star-filled sky. Even the poisoned air smelled sweeter then, or Barb imagined it did. These were moments to treasure, though she would never admit to such sentimental thoughts, even to her brother, Charlie. Or maybe, she told herself, especially to him.

She watched him now, on the roof of the Hammerhead, watched him on his hands and knees, working on her favorite bike. Bolts, chains, chrome and greasy metal parts were scattered all over the asphalt roof. No matter how often she watched him, she was always amazed at the way her brother's hands moved so swiftly over the big machine. It was like watching a sculptor fashion a likeness in steel. No one who didn't know him would ever imagine that behind Charlie Kopetski's dark lenses, there was nothing but ugly red scars.

Barb stood by a weathered brick chimney, gripping a glass of cold spring water in her hand. It was a beverage she didn't offer at the Hammerhead, and if she did, it was unlikely anyone would prefer it over rotgut whiskey and gin. Still, it was the most expensive drink in town – pure and totally clear, nothing floating in it at all. She had it smuggled in from France at two hundred bucks a quart.

"How's the head," Barb asked, "you feeling okay?"

"Doesn't hurt at all. I'm still drunk. That's why you sober people don't understand, love. It's not the drinking, it's the stopping that drags you down."

"I guess you could look at it that way."

"Trust me on this. Drinking's what I do."

"Charlie . . ."

Barb started to speak, then cut herself short. Nagging at her brother only drove them apart and didn't do a damn bit of good.

Maybe I'd be a boozer, too, if I had to live in darkness the rest of my life . . .

And that wasn't all of it, she knew. Some of the scars of war were on the inside; all of it didn't show. She and Charlie shared some of those.

"I did okay," she said, quickly moving to safer ground. "Don't have to worry about the payroll for a week. Made a good score." She paused for a healthy swallow of imported water. "Conned old Rhino Schmitz into payin' me double for that bail-jumper. Rhino almost had a stroke. Hell, worse than that. He almost stood up."

Charlie laughed. He turned his face toward her and gave her a wicked grin. "You talking about who I think you're talking about? That guy Willis is after? You got it backwards, little sister. Schmitz conned *you*."

Barb blinked. "What?" What are you trying to tell me, Charlie? Just get it out, okay?"

"Guess you didn't know. A very pretty lady who

61

does a lot of business on the street knows this cop who knows somebody else, right? This Krebs was no ordinary bail-jumper. He was *Resistance*, Barb."

"So? Willis told me that."

"So something big's going down. There is a one-million-dollar Congressional bounty on this dude."

Barb moaned. "A million bucks? *Why?*"

"Hey, who knows?"

"Damn." Barb slammed a fist into her open palm. "No wonder Schmitz was such an easy touch. He gives me twenty thousand, turns Krebs over to the Congressional goons for a mil. Nice return on the day."

Barb let out a breath. "That son of a bitch, Willis. He knew about the bounty too."

Charlie reached for a wrench, felt it, put it down and found the right size.

"I know what you're thinking, Barb. Don't. That money's gone You want to forget this one, leave it alone."

"Who said I was going to do anything, Charlie? You hear me say that?"

"I know you pretty well, little sister."

"Don't call me that. I'm two years older than you."

"You don't tell anybody, I won't either."

Barb laughed. "I'm getting something to eat. You want to leave that mess for a while?"

Charlie paused, set down his wrench, then shook his head. "I mean it, Barb. This one's got sticky all over it. Offing cops is serious shit. Even in Steel Harbor."

Barb made a noise in her throat. "Those weren't cops, Charlie, none of those thugs are cops, they're hired goons."

"They're goons with a badge," he told her. "Pin a star on a dead dog and it's a cop, far as the law's concerned."

"Yeah, well." Barb stretched and yawned. "Anybody asks, I'm not losing any sleep. You stayin' or coming down?"

"Staying, I guess. I can't see it, but I can feel it when the sun comes up. I like to know it's still there."

Barb looked at him. There was only one male on the planet she cared anything about, and he was sitting right there in a tangle of greasy parts. She wished she could tell him that and didn't know how.

"Well don't screw my bike up," she said, "they're hard to get now."

Charlie didn't answer. Barb walked back down, thinking about a bath and bed. She'd seen the sun before. It would look just like it always did . . .

4:46 a.m. – Riot call, Westway and 9th:
Officer arrived upon scene to discover
approximately twenty-five (25) citizens
engaged in violence concerning possession of
contents of three (3) GUU (Garbage Utility
Units). Nine minor injuries, four treated by
Med-Aid. SHAM (Steel Harbor Auxiliary
Maintenance) dispatched to scene. Crowd
dispersed.

**5:22 a.m. – Officer observation, 900 block,
S. 233rd St.:**
Upon routine patrol, this officer observed
two members of UNFISH (United Nations
Forces in Steel Harbor) engaged in ID check
activities at Border Station 32. Two citizens
dismissed. Three citizens held for DED
(Direct Emergency Detainment), resulting in
two major injuries, one accidental death.

6:09 a.m. – Assault call, 20006 Cherry Lane:
Officer arrived on scene to discover
approximately nineteen (19) citizens between
the ages of eight and eleven, engaged in
slashing and robbing one male citizen, aged
78. Weapons used: Hatchets. Assailants fled
at officer's approach. Distinctive jackets
bearing the images of headless male and
female torsos, accompanied by the legend:
DEKAPITATURS (improper spelling),
enabled this officer to identify perpetrators as
possible street-gang members.
    Male victim sustained multiple cuts and

abrasions about head and body. Med-Aid units arrived to assist. One (1) hatchet, steel, with wooden handle, retrieved at scene.

7:15 a.m. – Officer observation:
Two (2) deceased and disemboweled Snakers at the corner of Fifth and Apple. SHAM dispatched to scene.

8:00 a.m. – Officer off-duty:

[The above is excerpted from the report of a Steel Harbor police officer (name unknown).]

– Johnny Gray Wolf, PhD, *Fall From Glory* (2032), University of the New Sioux Nation Press.

Eleven

Not for the first time, Barb wondered why in hell she'd ever gotten into the bar business. You had to be mentally deficient, suicidal and totally devoid of any pride or self-respect. The Hammerhead hadn't been open half an hour and there had already been an electrical fire in the kitchen, two fistfights in the bar and a drug OD in the ladies' room. Besides that, the lead guitarist of Organ Transplant had been beaten senseless by UN goons the night before. What next, Barb wondered – nuclear attack?

Curly caught her eye from across the room and nodded toward the door. Barb looked and let out a sigh. Terrific. Start of a perfect evening. Police Chief Willis stood in the entry way, resplendent in a white formal uniform. Black jackboots, riding pants, tight jacket with silver-tasseled epaulets, silver piping everywhere. His white and silver officer's cap was too large for his head. Colorful medals adorned his chest. Barb was certain he'd awarded them to himself: coercion, sexual harassment, assault and bribery in the line of fire. With his scarecrow frame he looked like a six-foot roach – not the kind you squash, the kind you smoke.

Barb waited until Curly led Willis to his table – "Best in the house," he said, the same thing he said to everyone.

"Champagne for the jerk-off cop," Barb told a waiter. "The cheap stuff with the French label. On *his* tab."

The waiter nodded. Barb pasted on a smile and walked over to greet the chief.

"My, don't we look nice. What's with the monkey suit?"

Willis looked annoyed. "Not my usual *working* wear, of course. You know how uniforms impress the Congressionals. The delegation got here this morning. My captain says they've stuck their nose in everything. You'd think we don't know how to –"

Willis caught himself and brushed an invisible mote of dust off his sleeve. "I told you about this, Barb. You ought to listen sometime. This is important to me and to Steel Harbor as well."

"'Course it is," Barb said. "I could hardly sleep last night."

Willis was too distracted to catch the dig. He glanced nervously at the door. "I trust you appreciate the fact that I'm bringing these . . . distinguished persons here. I could take them anywhere."

"Hey, what the hell do you want? I'm overwhelmed."

"Make sure you are. And make damn certain no . . . unfortunate incidents take place while my guests are on the premises. I would not appreciate that."

"Here?" Barb spread her hands. "What could happen?"

Willis scowled. "This isn't funny. I hope you don't think – think that you –"

The chief bit his lip and stared past Barb. Barb

turned and saw a short, heavy man with shaggy brows and deep-set eyes. His uniform made Willis's elaborate get-up look like a doorman's outfit. It was black as night and studded with enough gold to buy every whore in Steel Harbor twice.

Only this one, Barb thought, *wouldn't ever have to pay. He'd take what he wanted and wouldn't stop to ask.*

Willis nearly upset his table, jumping up to greet his guests.

"Arf! Arf!" Barb said at his back. She laughed and walked over to the bar. Charlie was standing there holding his drink. As she approached, his chin jerked up, his shades reflecting the Hammerhead's colored lights.

"How many of 'em? Five, six – what?"

Barb raised a brow. "You scare me sometimes. How do you do that?"

"Radar," Charlie said. "And a good nose. You'd be surprised the things I smell in the course of a night in here."

"Yeah, well *I* can smell these jokers and I don't have any special knack at all. Seven of them, to answer your question. Congressional storm-trooper types. Six gorillas and the head goon. Head guy looks like an overfed rat. Bad skin, killer eyes."

"Pryzer," Charlie said.

"Who?"

"Colonel Victor Pryzer. Very bad news. He likes to kill people, and he likes to do it slow."

Barb made a face. "He better not kill anybody in *my* place. We got rules in here."

Charlie downed his drink. His blind eyes never left

the far end of the room. "I think I'll run upstairs and bake a cake. I've got a couple of anti-tank mines I've been saving for a special occasion."

"Behave yourself. This is an apolitical bar."

"Speak for yourself," Charlie said.

Barb gave him a look and strolled back to talk to the chef. The guys from DC were likely used to real steak, and they wouldn't go for dog.

"Alexander Willis," the chief grinned, "Director of Police Operations here in Steel Harbor. It's a great pleasure to welcome you, sir."

Pryzer looked at Willis's outstretched hand with disgust.

"Listen, and listen good, you little shit." Pryzer leaned down until his eyes were an inch from Willis' nose. "Wipe that stupid smile off your face, *Chief*. This burned-out hellhole is the last place on earth I want to be. If it wasn't for your complete incompetence I wouldn't *have* to be here in the first place, would I? Do you *hear* me, mister?"

Willis blinked. Pryzer's breath would wilt a dinosaur, but the chief didn't dare back off.

"Yes, well I had hoped, Colonel, to have Krebs and Cora D. in custody and extradited to Washington by now. As you know, we encountered a . . . certain degree of difficulty."

"Are you listening? I don't think you're listening to me." Pryzer poked a stubby finger in Willis's chest. "If Corrina Devonshire gets away, I will personally pull your heart out of your ass and stuff it down your throat. You follow me?"

"I think I get it yeah. I think I understand that."

"Good, good!" Pryzer's muddy eyes sparkled and his face broke into a grin. "Then let's enjoy ourselves, right?" He slapped Willis on the back. "How do you get a drink in this dump, anyway?"

Willis turned away quickly and led Pryzer and his entourage to his table. He wanted to reach up and wipe the trickle of sweat off his brow, but he knew Pryzer would see. God, those eyes! Willis had seen a lot of awful shit in his life, but he'd never seen anything like the things that lived in Pryzer's eyes.

Pryzer sat.

The instant his butt hit the chair, his goons sat too. Willis thought they all looked alike. None of them spoke. Talking wasn't what they did. They had other things to do. Willis had some men like that who worked for him, but he suspected that none of them could match this crew.

He glanced up, relieved to see Barb approaching the table.

"Colonel Pryzer," he said, tossing his napkin aside and hopping to his feet, "may I present our hostess, Miss Bar –"

"No need, Willis," Pryzer cut him off. "Even up in Washington we've heard of Barb Wire."

"Charmed," Barb said.

Pryzer bent to kiss her hand. Barb smiled and repressed a shudder. It felt as if a snake's tongue had brushed against her fingers.

"An interesting establishment you have here, Miss Wire." Pryzer looked her over, assaulted her with his eyes. "You attract a real eclectic clientele."

Barb shrugged. "Steel Harbor attracts all kinds of unconventional types. Some of 'em drift in here."

"Yeah, I expect they do." Pryzer showed her a grisly smile. "Rumor has it you used to hang out with those – how'd you put it now? – unconventional types. That you used to fight with the scum likes to call themselves the Resistance."

Barb tossed her hair over her shoulders. "Now, I bet you hear a *lot* of rumors in your position, Colonel. You don't want to believe everything you hear."

"You're right. And I certainly don't."

"I didn't think you did. Why, if you people up in DC took the time to listen to rumors you wouldn't get *anything* done, would you?"

Willis choked on his drink. Pryzer's raw face turned a brilliant shade of red, then he quickly brought himself under control. He laughed at Barb's joke, turned to his goons, and the goons laughed too.

"Colonel, what I guess you don't know," Barb said, leaning her hands on the table and granting him a lovely view, "is that I'm strictly neutral as far as the current conflict is concerned. Essentially I'm a businesswoman."

Pryzer reluctantly moved his gaze off Barb's cleavage. "Then we could, ah, maybe do some business. I'm sure we'd both enjoy that."

Barb pretended not to understand. Pryzer snapped his fingers for another round of drinks.

"I'll get to the point," he told her. "There is a fugitive – a damned *traitor* – at large in Steel Harbor. She intends to try escaping into Canada with the help of some of the more . . . uninformed and disenchanted citizens of this city."

Barb shrugged. "Do I look disenchanted, Colonel?

71

Hey, I'm as enchanted as anyone."

Pryzer ignored her. "This person's name is Dr. Corrina Devonshire. You might've heard of her as Cora D.." He snorted in disgust. "These misguided rebels think up real romantic names for their trashy leaders." He gave Willis a chilling look. "Sort of mystic-like, you know. Helps keep their big legend alive."

"Well, you know how people are," Barb said.

Pryzer's tiny eyes nearly closed. "No, how are they, Miss Wire?"

Barb didn't have to answer. The waiters arrived with sizzling steaks. Barb glanced at them, saw they were genuine Canadian beef, or close enough.

Pryzer waited until the waiters were gone, then dropped a pair of color photographs on the table.

"We're not sure what she looks like, of course. She's had her face fixed up – you know, surgically altered. She doesn't look like she used to anymore."

Barb batted her eyes. "Boy, I bet it's hard to find somebody when you don't know what they look like, huh?"

"Who the hell cares what she looks like?" Pryzer waved her words away. "We've got scientific stuff to handle that. We got the best. Retinal screening'll give you a positive ID of *every* citizen. You can look like – like him," Pryzer said, jabbing a finger at Chief Willis. "Doesn't matter, we'd know it was you."

"I'm not sure I care for the comparison," Barb said.

"Listen, Miss Wire –" God, she was a looker, Pryzer thought. He imagined her bound, totally restrained. Hooked up to the shiny silver wires somewhere. And not in a goddam auto parts store this time . . .

72

"Miss Wire, I want to assure you that in spite of your levity this is a real serious matter. I'd take it . . . kindly if the Congressional Army could count on your help and cooperation."

"Let me just say that the Steel Harbor police have complete confidence in Miss Wire," Willis added, looking desperately at Barb. "In the past we've worked very close in a number of – huh?"

Curly scurried up to the table wearing his 'Intense Emergency Look: Number Three'.

"Icemaker, boss. It's on the blink again. I've got glacier city back there."

"Excuse me, gentlemen," Barb said, "I've got a bar to run. I swear, this *always* happens when I'm just getting started having fun."

Pryzer opened his mouth to protest. Curly weaved through the crowd and Barb vanished in his wake.

"Real interestin' woman. I expect she can be useful to us. You sure you got a handle on her, Willis?"

"Oh, yes, absolutely, Colonel. No question."

A bead of sweat perched on the end of Willis's nose. He brought his napkin up fast and faked a sneeze. *Why had be brought Pryzer to the Hammerhead in the first place?* he wondered. *What was he thinking of? Why hadn't he just slit this throat instead?*

He wondered how hard it would be to have Barb dumped in the river. *Maybe he could do it before Pryzer learned what kind of help she could give . . . the five hundred ways she could look like an angel, steal you blind, and make your life a living hell?*

Twelve

Lightning split the night sky and rain drummed down on the armored roof of the cab. Dr. Corrina Devonshire decided she'd kill Axel hood if he ever got her out of Steel Harbor alive. The thought seemed to strike her as she clutched the filthy seat, squeezed her eyes shut and waited for the driver to hit the big semi head on. He didn't have brakes and he didn't have lights. He had a gas pedal and a horn and faith in his ancient Mayan gods.

"Listen, I'm sorry," Axel said. "You're not comfortable with this, I can tell."

"My God, on top of all your other sterling qualities you're perceptive as well." Corrina slid down in her seat and waited for the next hair-raising encounter on the street. "No, I am *not* comfortable in this death-trap. I'm scared out of my wits."

"It's not perfect, I'll admit," Axel said. "But believe me, it's the safest way to travel in Steel Harbor."

"And what are the *un*safe ways?"

"Any conveyance that's open. Anything that won't handle concussion up to Impact Three. Anything that has tires that go flat. Anything that –"

"All right, I apologize. I didn't realize I was going first class."

"Huh-uh." Axel shook his head. "First class is the M-2000 AAV – Armored Attack Vehicle. Now *that's* first class. Only the Congressionals have all of those."

"I don't think they're likely to loan one to me," Corrina said.

She couldn't imagine she'd ever be grateful to breathe the outdoor air again. Still, after the unbelievable odors of the cab, the night's warm toxic breeze was a pleasant relief.

The storm had rumbled off to the south when they stepped out of the cab. Corrina felt a moment of sudden panic as she was swallowed up in the crowd, smothered by a writhing mass of Feelers, Woollies and Cranks. A whole array of new smells assailed her senses. Fear and bad breath. Wet hair and sweat. And, overpowering all else, the cloying odor of cloves.

Lord help us, Corrina thought, most of these people are high on Karachi Ice! She couldn't believe that fearsome drug had made its way over here, or that anyone was dumb enough to use it. Some fool in a high-school chemistry class had stumbled on it in Pakistan and killed half the country's population before they shut down the source.

"It's modified now," Axel said, watching her sniff the air. "Toned down quite a bit."

"That's nice. You mean it doesn't kill people anymore?"

"Oh, sure. It just doesn't kill 'em *fast*."

Axel worked his way through the crowd to the front of the line, Corrina hanging on his arm for dear life. Axel knew from experience bouncers were too smart for paper money. There was too much bad stuff around. He slipped the man a gold Irish doubloon and was ushered right in.

Corrina waited while Axel checked his gun. The cab, the dark alleyways, were suddenly looking good.

"I don't like this place," she said. "I don't like it at all."

"I don't either," he told her, "but we don't have a lot of choice. Relax, will you? No one has the slightest idea who you are. Your own mother wouldn't recognize you now."

"You don't know my mother," Corrina said.

Axel opened the door from the lobby. The blare of music hit Corrina like a blow. A waiter muttered something she couldn't hear and guided them through the crowd. Everybody looked blue in the pulsating lights. She saw a half-naked woman with bright red mohawk hair, a man in tight leather with a leash around his neck. There were girls in silver masks, men in silky hose.

As they passed a large table on a raised dais, Corrina held her breath. Six black-clad troopers sat side by side. In the center of the group was a man in black and gold. He glanced up as she passed, slashed her with his eyes and looked away.

"Axel," she said, squeezing his arm, "there are Congressionals in here. *Fascists*."

"Relax."

"Don't tell me that again. Don't you ever tell me that again."

"Yeah, right." Axel nodded and sat, and the waiter pulled a chair out for Corrina. Axel ordered drinks.

Corrina looked around and licked her lips. "Listen, I appreciate what you're doing, don't think I don't.

76

But my neck is in the noose here, so to speak. I think it's time you gave a clue. Who are we meeting here? I want to know, Axel, and I want to know now."

"A woman."

"That's very helpful. What kind of woman exactly?"

"A woman I used to know."

Corrina frowned. "Why is it you don't sound all that sure to me?"

"Sure of what?"

"Sure of *her*, Axel. Whoever she happens to be."

Axel shrugged and studied the room. "It was a long time ago."

"Okay."

"Things change. People do too."

"Oh, fine."

"What?"

"I don't like the sound of that. Things and people changing. That doesn't sound very hopeful to me."

He looked at her then, at the skin drawn tight around her face, at the tension that strained every muscle in her body.

"I wish you could . . . get a little rest before we go on with all this," he said gently. "You look like you're about to come apart."

He reached out and touched her hand. She smiled and drew it back. "I've been three years on the run, friend. I can wait one more day to rest."

"Yeah, sure," Axel said. He stood, let his gaze sweep the crowded dance floor, the big bar beyond. "Okay, this is it. Wait here and pretend you're having a great time."

"Just explain it to her rationally. People respond best to reason, I've found."

Axel rolled his eyes. "*That* comment could only come from a person who's never met Barb Wire." He kissed her on the forehead and made his way across the room.

Pushing through the dancers, he made it safely to the bar. People were lined up three deep, but Axel had a knack for getting where he wanted to be. Squeezing in next to an American sergeant, he ordered a bourbon straight up. The bartender nodded, poured on the run, and slid the glass down the bar.

Axel took a satisfying whiff, raised the glass to his lips, and froze. A tall, willowy blonde with sleepy eyes was giving him a look that went all the way down to his belly. She was absolutely breathtaking, slick and fine from head to toe.

"Hi," Axel said, "my name's Axel, and I just got in town."

"Hi yourself," the beauty said. "Raymond's the name, and gasoline's the game."

Axel's face fell. "Yeah, well – fine . . . See you around some time."

He grabbed his drink and backed off, moving quickly down the bar. "Man, you've been out of touch too long," he muttered to himself. "Straighten up, Axel, or you'll get yourself in trouble in here."

His glass was nearly empty. He'd downed the first drink like a man coming out of the desert. He was debating whether to push his way back to the bar when he spotted Charlie, not ten feet away. His throat went tight at the sight of the slightly bowed shoulders, the stony profile. The past was bad enough to think about. Meeting it face to face was something else.

Taking a deep breath, he walked up behind Charlie

and stood there a long moment before he spoke.

"Hello, Charlie. It's been a little while . . ."

Charlie went rigid. He sat down his drink and turned his dark shades on Axel Hood.

"Must be one of those . . . Post Traumatic Stress flashbacks. I could swear I heard an old ghost from the battlefield."

Axel tried to ignore the bitterness, the touch of anger in Charlie's voice.

"Okay, so I didn't send a Christmas card. So you're surprised to see me."

Charlie paused a moment, then reached up and lifted his glasses. "What do you think, Axel? Do I look surprised? How do I look to you?"

A chill touched the back of Axel's neck. Where Charlie's eyes used to be there were now only red puckered scars.

"Jesus," Axel said.

"Guess you didn't *hear*. Got these courtesy of a Congressional land mine. One of the new carbon-fiber jobs. Very effective, too. Montana border conflict. Two years ago."

"I'm sorry, Charlie." It seemed a lame thing to say.

"Yeah? Me too."

Axel signaled the bartender. "Two Wild Turkeys. The real stuff."

The bartender glanced at Charlie, then gave Axel a look.

"You don't have to buy me a drink, Axel. I'm real tight with the management. Hell, I'm – real tight, period." Charlie laughed at himself. "I'm in the enviable position of a man who can get all the booze he can drink."

Axel looked at him, saw the line of his jaw, the rigid set of his mouth. Charlie was still young, but the red complexion, the broken veins of the hard drinker, were already making their mark. He wondered if Charlie ever came close to sober anymore.

"You've got a lot of nerve coming in here, Axel. Hell of a lot of nerve." Charlie sniffed his drink and made a face as if there might be something unpleasant in his glass. "There's a – a lot of places you could drink in Steel Harbor besides the Hammerhead."

"I need to see Barb, Charlie. That's why I'm here. I guess you maybe figured that."

Charlie frowned and ran a hand through his hair. "I don't know if . . . talking to Barb's such a good idea, you know? She took that business at Seattle a little bit harder than I did, pal."

Axel leaned in close, talking against the blare of the music.

"I need her help. I've got to get in touch with the Resistance." He gripped his glass, tried to find Corrina across the floor, and couldn't see her anywhere. "It's important, Charlie. Real important."

"Haven't you heard, man? Barb's retired. She isn't into that line of work anymore." Charlie downed his drink. He grinned at some private joke and shook his head. "If I was – if I was you, I'd leave while I was ahead. She sees you in here –"

Charlie stopped. A sound from Axel told his heightened senses all he needed to know.

"Uh-oh. Too late, right? 'Scuse me while I . . . get outta the line of fire."

Charlie laughed and walked off down the bar,

slightly out of step and definitely out of synch with the world.

Axel saw her coming halfway across the room, saw the signs, the movements, the body language he knew so well. He could almost feel the heat in her eyes, the rage that smoldered there. It was a wild and unreasonable thought, but just to make sure he looked her over quickly to see if she was armed.

"Hello, Barb. I know this is –"

She stepped up close, slapped him so hard his ears rang.

Axel took a breath. "Okay, fine. I guess I had that one coming."

"You guess? You *guess*?" Barb squeezed her fists at her sides. "Get out. Get out of here, you son of a bitch!"

"Barb, listen to me. I need your help –"

"Rot in hell, Axel."

"Yeah. I'm sure I will. Later. Right now I need to talk. Charlie says you're out of the movement now. I don't believe that."

"Believe it. Get *out* of here, Axel. Now!"

Barb turned and stalked off. Axel reached out and grabbed her arm. Barb thrust out her jaw in defiance; her eyes went dark with anger. Axel didn't budge. He gripped her tighter and forced her up close against his chest.

"Look at me and tell me that," he said. "Look at me! Tell me you gave up, that you forgot what happened out there, that you forget everything you believed in."

"That part of me is dead, Axel." She spat out the words and jerked away. "Dead along with every other part of me you killed. My God . . ." She stared at him in wonder. "Am I supposed to *forget* about all that, just . . . toss it aside like nothing ever happened?"

"No, I don't guess you can. I don't suppose I expect you to. All I'm asking is you forget it for a couple of minutes, damn it, and listen to me."

Barb gave him a harsh laugh. "Oh, right. Where have I heard this before?"

Axel looked past her. People were starting to watch, curious about what was going on. They all knew who Barb Wire was, but they didn't know him.

"You've got to know that the last thing I'd ever do is come to you and . . . ask something from you."

"Good. I'm glad you know that, 'cause the last thing *I'd* ever do is –"

Axel glared. "This is important. Damn it, will you trust me on this!"

Barb's voice shook. Seeing him again, hurling her back into the past, was almost more than she could take.

"Trust you? You mean, like I did in Seattle?" She fought to settle herself, to keep from letting go. "That's the wrong approach, Axel. Trust is not exactly the way to get to me anymore."

She was walking away from him now, past the bar toward the door to the kitchen. Axel kept up with her, matching her step for step.

"What happened in Seattle is . . . not what you think. I never intended to hurt you. Things happen in the middle of a goddamn war, Barb. Things we can't –"

Barb whirled around to face him. "Get out of here,

Axel. Do it now." Her voice was almost soft, deadly calm. *"Get out of here and don't even think about coming back . . ."*

Axel stared at her, startled by what he saw. He thought he knew every side of her, every shade of passion and anger, but he'd never seen the fury, the outright hatred he saw there now.

"Barb, for God's sake – !" The words caught in his throat. He searched for some look that might betray her, might tell him that everything they'd had wasn't gone. There was nothing – nothing but the aching beauty of a woman he no longer knew, a woman who lashed him with cold and distant eyes, then turned and stalked away.

She watched him from where she stood, half hidden by the crowd. He dropped some bills on his table, bent to speak to the woman. The woman looked frightened, confused. She stood and followed him quickly out the door.

My God she's lovely, Barb thought. *Who the hell is she and what's she doing with him?*

Barb felt the color rise to her face. What difference did it make who Axel Hood was with? That part of her life was flat *over*, dead and forgotten.

Damn you, Axel . . . why did you have to come back here?

Reports from our observers in the American West War Zone (AWWZ) confirm those rumors of a fierce new battle on the Eastern Nebraska front. At approximately noon (CDT) yesterday, armored units of the Congressional Third Army, under the command of Major General Garner 'Hacksaw' Marcos, launched a surprise attack on the besieged American Eleventh Corps in the Omaha Perimeter.

A rapid pincer movement across the Platte drove the American forces back across the Missouri in a chaotic and disastrous retreat. Many units were stranded on the Nebraska shore without support. While details are sparse at this time, it is clear that casualties were extremely heavy, especially on the American side. Not since the Second Gettysburg last summer have so many men died in a single engagement.

Congressional General Marcos stated, "Brave men fight hard, whether their cause is just or not. I cannot express my grief at this unnecessary loss of life. I can only pray this tragedy will convince other misguided officers and men to lay down their arms and bring our beleaguered nation together once again . . ."

[Excerpt from the *Winnipeg Post-Dispatch*, the day following the Battle of the Bloody Missouri.]

- Johnny Gray Wolf, PhD, *Fall From Glory* (2032), University of the New Sioux Nation Press.

Thirteen

Axel didn't dare look at Corrina. Corrina could see right through him. One glance would tell her he was scared out of his wits and he didn't think she ought to know that. She needed to know that he was cool, calm and mean as rusty nails, a fearless leader of men.

"Are you all right?" Corrina asked. "You okay?"

Axel jumped as she touched his arm. "Of course I'm okay, why would you think I'm not okay. I'm just fine."

Corrina gave him a curious look. "I'm just asking, Axel, because I'm *not*. I'm scared out of my shoes if you want to know."

"Hey, just take it easy, there's not a – not a thing to be afraid of." Axel squeezed her shoulder. "I'm right here."

"I know where you are. What I'd like to know is where I'm going."

"I'm working on it," he said.

Axel moved to the head of the alley and studied the street. There was nothing to see. Wet paving stones, hollow buildings and an avalanche of trash. Which didn't mean there was nothing out there. He knew, from experience, what you didn't see in Steel Harbor was what you had to worry about. That's what was likely watching *you*.

And that was real peculiar, he thought. He'd never

felt like this in combat, hunkered down on a cold hillside or in a pile of ruins somewhere. You were scared out there, sure, you'd be stupid if you weren't. But this was a different kind of scared – you knew who your enemy was and you knew what he could do. Not here, though. You didn't know who the hell was after you here. And they seldom looked like soldiers with helmets and guns. They looked like grannies and ten-year-old kids. They looked like housewives and bums.

They were two blocks from the Hammerhead, next to a gutted shoe store. Axel had tried to get a cab, but all of them were busy whisking the lowlifes and the highrollers from one debauchery to the next. Corrina hadn't wanted to wait; she didn't like standing there with people gawking at her. People with tattoos on their lips, people with things stuck up their nose.

Axel said absolutely no, they'd wait for a cab to get free. He said only two kinds of people walked around in Steel Harbor, the killers and their prey.

And right after that, after he'd told her they'd have to stand and wait, that was the moment when he had the awful feeling that someone was watching, that someone was there, that they weren't safe at all, not even in the middle of a crowd. His sense of danger was so strong, so intense, that it overcame his caution at once. He grabbed Corrina's hand and led her quickly away from the neon brightness of the Hammerhead's sign, and into the darkened streets.

Now, standing at the head of the alley, he was no longer sure that he'd done the right thing. The feeling was still there, stronger than ever now, but so was the sense that no one in his right mind would be wandering around here at night . . .

"Axel," Corrina said softly, "if there's something you think you ought to tell me, I'd be pleased if you'd go ahead and do it. As a matter of fact, you'd by God *better* or I'm going to hit you with something right now."

"There's a lot I need to tell you," he said. "I'm just not sure where to start."

"Try me. A lot of people say I'm real quick."

Axel checked the streets once more. "The woman I was talking to, Barb Wire, she and I – she and I used to be close. She's –"

"I *know* who she is." Corrina looked at him. "You and Barb Wire?"

"Yeah. We were a happy couple for a while. Okay, I don't guess we were too damn happy, but we were a couple all the same."

"Okay . . ."

"And we're not a couple now. I mean, something happened and I won't go into that but back there I asked her to help and she told me to go to hell."

"I see."

"No, you don't, but, yeah, I guess you do. Part of it, anyway."

He turned and faced her. "Corrina, I'm sorry. I should never have gone in there, it was a lousy idea. I screwed up good. To be perfectly honest, I made a real mess of this."

"All right, Axel."

"*Please* don't say 'All right, Axel'. Will you not do that? It's not all right, it's not all right at all."

"What would you like me to say? Tell me and I'll try to say what it is you want to hear."

Her dark eyes caught a spark of light from the street. "What I don't think I can do is listen to this –

this 'I'm a bad guy' shit you're on right now. I don't want to hear what you can't do. I want to hear what you intend to do next!"

Axel stared at her. He almost laughed aloud, forgetting for a moment this was not the place for that.

"All right," he said, "I quit. You got me, friend."

"I trust you, Axel. You ought to know that. Try and trust yourself."

"That's the hard part sometimes."

"That's something I'd know about. I've had to learn it myself. These last few years in hiding, running from one place to the next . . . I've been ready to toss it all in a dozen times. I wouldn't like anyone to know it, but it's true."

Axel grinned. "You Resistance heroes are all alike. Modest to the core." He tried to see her face. "After Canada, then what? Where do you go from there?"

Corrina shook her head. "I don't ever think that far. It's been too long since I've had any choice what to do."

"Uh – huh. But if you did?"

"I can't answer that. Let's get me there first, then I'll try an –"

"*Don't anybody shoot. It's bad luck to kill the handicapped.*"

Axel jerked up straight, whipped the gun from under his jacket and swept Corrina aside.

Charlie's husky laugh came out of the shadows. "You're rusty man. In the bad old days you'd have known someone was out there."

"I did," Axel said, letting out a breath, "and you're right. I'm rusty as hell. What are you doing here, Charlie?"

"Hey, Axel . . ." Charlie tried to look hurt. "Is that any way to treat an old friend – even a friend who thinks you're a no-good son of a bitch?"

"Axel –"

Charlie turned his dark shades on Corrina. "I don't guess Axel's going to introduce me. The boy's uncouth. Never had the manners of a mongrel dog."

"This is Charlie Kopetski," Axel said. "Barb Wire's brother. This is an . . . acquaintance, Charlie."

"Hey, did I ask?" Charlie held up his palms. "Whoever you are, lady, your secret's safe with me. Ol' Charlie's blind as a bat. Blind as a . . . blind *drunk* bat, as a matter of fact."

He leaned against the wet alley wall, raised his head and sniffed the night air.

"Ah, Steel Harbor. Garden spot of this lovely nation." He turned to the pair again. "You nice people still looking for the Resistance? Charlie can help. Just don't tell Barb or she'll kick my skinny ass from here to Mexico . . ."

Fourteen

Axel didn't know where the car came from and didn't ask. It appeared ten minutes after Charlie Kopetski slipped into the night, making his way back to the Hammerhead with no help at all.

The car looked like the typical pre-war clunker, much like the one in which Axel and Corrina had nearly lost their lives moments after their arrival in town. Looks, though, were often deceiving, as Axel knew. The fading paint and crumpled fenders masked a first-class coat of armor. The taped and spidered windows were fake as well – hiding the best bullet-proof material money could buy. Or, in this case, the best the owners of this disreputable-looking wreck could steal.

The driver didn't move. The passenger got out quickly and efficiently patted down Axel and Corrina.

"I'm placing these sacks over your heads," he told them. "You will then kneel on the floor. You will bury your head in the seat with your hands behind your neck. I will be watching you at all times. If at any time I even imagine you are attempting to see any-thing but your own eyelids, I will shoot you in the head. Any questions?"

"Just one," Axel said. "Where did you serve, Sarge? Third Division or the Droppers?"

The driver stifled a laugh. The other man made a

sound of disgust, slammed the back door and got back in the front.

The car took off down the street, traveling at a moderate speed. Axel could tell from the rich, throaty sound of the engine that this particular "clunker" could likely take off and fly if the occasion should arise.

The ride seemed to last forever. Axel knew they were making a great many twists and turns, which meant they were going a great distance or riding in circles – practicing the standard procedure for throwing off a possible tail.

The driver hummed something that Axel didn't know. It was from an opera that he liked but he could never remember the name.

He wondered what Corrina was thinking about. Probably the same thing he was – whether Charlie Kopetski's friends were taking them to the Resistance or simply taking them for a ride. Either way, they wouldn't find out until they got out of the car. The men in charge were pros and there was no sense making a mess that you'd likely have to clean up yourself.

The car stopped.

The back door opened and the man said, "Out."

Axel and Corrina stretched their legs. The man pulled off their hoods. They might have been a block from where they started; the neighborhood looked much the same.

"Two doors down. There's a number says 'ten'. Go on inside. It'll be real dark. Keep walking. Don't worry, you won't run into anything."

The man got back in the car. Axel watched them vanish round a corner. He enjoyed listening to the engine. You didn't hear a lot of real good engines these days.

"I hope we can trust these people," Corrina said. "I don't guess we've got a lot of choice."

"No, I don't guess we do." Axel stopped before the door marked 'ten', hesitated, then slowly pushed it open. The man hadn't lied. Inside it was dark as a murderer's heart.

"It's narrow," he told her. "Like a hall of some kind. You can touch both walls. Keep close to me."

Corrina didn't need to hear that. She kept one hand on his shoulder, one hand on the wall.

"I get the idea you and Charlie have known each other for some time."

"Longer than that."

"He doesn't like you very much."

"Like you say, you're real quick, ma'am." Axel laughed softly, his voice muffled by the walls. "He doesn't dislike me. He hates my guts."

"That's very reassuring. I feel better now."

"Actually, you should. Charlie is a drunk, marginally psychotic and severely depressed. He is also one of the gutsiest and most honest men I've ever known. Charlie Kopetski keeps his word."

Corrina let out a breath. "I'm glad you told me that. I don't think I could . . . handle it, after all this time, if someone betrayed me again."

Axel knew better than to dig into that. He hadn't known her long, but long enough to read a great deal of her story in her eyes, in her voice, in the lines of her face. Corrina Devonshire was a strong and beautiful woman, but in her own way she was as scarred as any veteran of the war, as maimed as any pathetic Snaker who scraped down a dark alleyway. Nobody got out of the war in one piece, and Corrina had left some vital parts behind . . .

The hallway took a sharp right, then a left. By now, Axel was certain this maze had been built with a single purpose in mind . . . to make sure no one got through unless the proprietors of the place wanted them to. Friends had nothing to worry about. Others would be quietly dispatched and left to the rats. The rats were clearly there; Axel could hear them scuttling ahead and crawling behind the walls.

Maybe that's who'll win the war . . . maybe the rats are simply waiting till both sides wear each other down. When it's all nearly over, when the man-things are too weak to resist . . .

Corrina grabbed his arm and Axel nearly jumped out of his skin.

"Damn it, don't *do* that!"

"My, we're jumpy," she said.

"Yeah? Well, you're right, we certainly are."

"Say something again, Axel."

"What?"

"Just say something. Anything."

"Hello? Hello-hello-hello."

"Do you hear it? Your voice is different. It isn't absorbed by the walls anymore. We're coming to the end of this thing."

"Hello!" Axel tried again. "You're right. And it's cooler. I smell . . ."

"Stone," Corrina finished. "Wet stone. I've hidden in enough places like this to know the smell."

"Okay. Keep your hand on my shoulder. If it doesn't open up we'll –"

The light came on directly in their path, a searing beam bright as a small sun. Axel and Corrina covered their eyes and turned away. Another light stabbed them, then another, so close Axel could feel the heat.

"All right," he said, "we get the point, turn those goddamn things off!"

All the lights but one disappeared. Axel held Corrina close, squinted and tried to blink the spots away.

"Whoever you are, you win. We're unarmed. Your guys got my weapon and she hasn't got one. You already know that."

The bright beam dimmed. Axel and Corrina could see the walls. The high, vaulted ceiling had been hit by an artillery shell. The gaping wound had been crudely patched. There were rows of broken seats; rotten wooden paneling sagged from the walls. The few bits of carpet left on the floor had been soaked a hundred times and gnawed by rats.

Corrina gazed past the broken seats, up the long aisle. There was a raised desk there, still almost intact. Behind it, a statue leaned precariously in its niche, its marble head blown off. Once the figure had carried two scales. Now it only had one.

"It works real well for us," a voice from somewhere said. "The Congressionals have forgotten about courtrooms, bastards don't know what they're for. Now, what do you people want here? You got thirty seconds of talk. Make it short and make it good . . ."

Fifteen

Axel peered into the shadows. There were people all around him. He couldn't hear them, couldn't see them, but he knew they were there. It was something you learned in combat, a trick of the body and the mind. You learned it quick or you were dead. And, as Charlie had so kindly pointed out, he was a little rusty now.

"Charlie Kopetski sent us," Axel said, "but you're aware of that. You know who I am, too. Axel Hood. Formerly with the Rocky Mountain Volunteers, the Missouri Headhunters, couple of outfits after that. I was at Seattle when it fell. I made three drops in the Powder Rivers War. Charlie likely told you that, too."

Axel paused and glanced at Corrina. "There's something Charlie doesn't know, and that's who *this* is." He took a step back, left her standing there alone. "Who I am doesn't matter, this woman is why we're here. Her name is Cora D.."

He heard his words echo off the walls as the others picked up the name, said it to themselves and sent it in harsh and breathless whispers around the room.

And then suddenly they were there. One figure and then another, rising from the dark, from behind the judge's bench, from beneath the broken chairs. Half a hundred men and women, maybe more, and every one, young and old, with hard and weary eyes, every one with a weapon aimed straight at Axel's heart.

Two gaunt and hollow-eyed men stepped forward. One held a battered Congressional M-99. The other, the older of the pair, carried a small black instrument. Axel recognized it at once. It was a portable retinal scanner, a piece of equipment also liberated from the Congressionals.

A woman stepped in front of the two men. She was short, with dark and tangled hair, a woman who walked with an athlete's practiced grace. She wore a ragged scar down one arm and a gold ring in her nose. She also carried a Brazilian officer's Splatter-Nine and looked strong enough to use it.

She glanced at Axel, dismissed him at once, studied Corrina a long time. Finally she nodded at the older man. He walked up to Corrina and held the instrument to her face. Corrina didn't move. The scanner hummed. Green light blinked weakly on the side.

"*Ret-inal scan veri-fied . . . Dr. Corrina Devonshire . . . Four-Four-Seven-Niner-One . . .*"

The woman with the nose-ring drew in a breath. Her eyes went wide and she let the pistol drop at her side. The other shadowy figures came forward, staring at Corrina, circling her but keeping an almost reverent distance.

Axel saw the awe, the wonder in their eyes. They had very little to hold on to in their fight against oppression, against overwhelming odds – no medals, no stones to mark their graves. Now a legend had appeared in their midst and they could scarcely believe their eyes.

"Cora D., I'm – we're honored." The woman

stepped forward and held out her hand. "Honest to God, I never thought I'd get to meet you in the flesh. I mean . . ." The woman shook her head and grinned. "Look, I'm not real good at this. I'm sort of the commander here. My name is Spike." She made a face. "It's a kind of dumb name, but – hey, what the hell?"

Corrina gripped her hand and smiled. "You're so young to have such a heavy responsibility, Spike. That tells me you must be pretty good."

Spike colored at that. "Yeah, I am. I guess. And I'm tough, too."

A few of the others laughed.

"She is, for a fact," one of the men said. "Got that name of hers froggin' a car full of Congressional sleazos." He made a gesture with his hand, a gut-slice straight across his belly.

"Wasn't a carful," Spike said, "for God's sake, Pete."

"Well, damn near."

When the woman turned half away Axel saw a hand-made Bowie knife fully eighteen inches long stuck in the back of her belt. It that was a 'frogger' he imagined it worked just fine.

Spike introduced Axel and Corrina to her crew, names Axel instantly forgot. She gave them the five-dollar tour of the ruins, showing them the judge's chamber, the meeting rooms and endless hallways that now served as storage rooms, dormitories and a small armory. There were people taking weapons apart, putting them back together, cannibalizing five guns to make one that worked.

Axel was depressed at the sight. These people were

97

so proud of what they were doing, so fiercely devoted, and had every right to be. Still, he wondered, what difference did it make? He'd fought with the Resistance before, and with an American army stronger and better equipped than any underground unit could ever hope to be . . . and the Congressionals had beat the crap out of every fighting unit they'd ever faced. They simply had too many weapons, too many men. They could *waste* half their equipment, sacrifice their men in some minor, unimportant skirmish, and still come out on top.

So why are these people fighting, why don't they quit? Okay, why didn't you, Axel, what's your excuse?

They sat around the battered table, Spike, Axel and Corrina, drinking weak coffee and eating stale sandwiches. Spike peeled an apple with her frogger, an awesome sight to see – like peeling a grape with a machete, Axel thought, though the woman could likely handle that as well.

"We knew you were coming," Spike said, "we knew you were trying to get out of the country, but we didn't know why and I'm not asking, okay?"

Spike shook her head in frustration. "We didn't know a hell of a lot, actually. Like *when* you were supposed to get here, or how."

"It wasn't easy," Corrina said. "The people who picked us up at the harbor –"

"Yeah, we know about that." Spike made a face. "I mean, we know *now*. Those boobies were from Brooker's cell. If it'd been my people nothing like that would've happened."

Axel gave her a curious look. "This Brooker . . . he knows about you, knows your group is here?"

"I know what you're thinking. Somebody knew you were coming; they knew where and when. We didn't. Brooker's people did. They run a loose ship over there, which is why I wouldn't give them the time of day. One of Brooker's people got caught. When that happens you talk, whether you want to or not. They put you on that goddamn mind machine . . ." Spike looked grim. "After that, Brooker should have had the sense to get to you, warn you off. He took a chance, nearly got you two caught, and lost two more of his people.

"Anyway, to answer your question: no. Brooker knows about us, but he doesn't know where we are. And he sure as hell never will, as long as I'm running this freak show."

Corrina gave Spike a sad and knowing look. "It happens all over, I'm afraid. There are underground cells that are more useful to the Congressionals than they are to us. Worse than that, we've uncovered several groups that had been entirely *taken over* by Congressional agents."

"My God." Spike shuddered at the thought. "I . . . didn't know that. You don't suppose Brooker –"

"No, I think you read him right. What did you call his people? Boobies, that's right. You don't have to be a traitor to get people killed. All you have to be is dumb."

Spike sipped at her coffee, set it down and gave the two a thoughtful look. "There's something you need to know. I should have told you sooner, but I thought there was maybe some better way to get to it . . . Okay, there isn't. We found Krebs. Not too long ago."

"That's – that's wonderful!" Corrina gripped the edge of the table. "Did you –"

"No. Wonderful it's not. Krebs is dead. We found his body stuffed in an abandoned washing machine behind the old VA hospital."

Spike stood and turned away. "The lenses were gone. Whoever killed him cut his eyeballs out. Left a couple of bloody sockets is all."

"Oh, boy," Axel said.

"The Congressionals have the lenses?" Corrina asked. "They did this?"

"No. That's the only good news. The Congressionals are still looking for Krebs. We know that for sure. Chief Willis and the local heat don't know squat either. Everybody's chasing their tails."

"Terrific," Axel said, "so who's got the lenses now? Anybody we know?"

"Not for sure, no. Word on the street is Krebs was snagged by a bounty hunter and turned over to a scumball bail bondsman named Rhino Schmitz. Schmitz was going to turn Krebs over to the Congressionals for the million-dollar tag on his head. But then he got wise to the lenses somehow."

Axel studied the ceiling. Something had scorched it with intense heat, and the paint hung in tortured flakes. "Sure he did. Those lenses are worth two, three times that much on the black market. They can beat any retinal scanning device anywhere."

"Spike, I have to have those lenses." Corrina leaned over and squeezed the young woman's hand. "Without them I'll never get past the checkpoint to get on that plane to Canada. I've *got* to have them."

"Then let's get to this Schmitz character," Axel said, "he's our best –"

Spike cut him off. "I'm afraid it's not that easy. We can't find him anywhere."

"That plane leaves in twenty-four hours," Corrina said. "There's got to be something we can do."

"There's only one person in this hellhole who has connections on all sides of the fence," Spike said. "If anybody would know how to dig through this mess, she would. The tricky part is, she doesn't give a damn about politics. And even if she would help, she doesn't do *anything* for free."

"Oh, shit . . ." Axel groaned and ran a hand over his eyes.

"You're going to have to talk to her again," Corrina said. "There's nothing else to do."

"Yeah, there is. Just shoot me in the head right now and get it over with . . ."

Sixteen

"You bend another card," Max said, "I'm bendin' you, man. I don't like playing cards with no one they're alla time bendin' cards, you know? I don't like doin' that."

"You're nuts," Arnie said. "I ain't bendin' no cards, I haven't ever bent a card in my life. You ask anyone, I ain't ever bent no friggin' cards."

"That's a lie an' you know it." Max doubled his big fists. "You deal me a card, you're going to bend it, you're goin' ta do it ever' time."

"Hell I am."

"Hell you ain't!"

"Shut up, the both of ya!" Pete stood and tossed his cards on the table. "You guys a coupla morons or what? I got to sit in this dump all day, I don't gotta listen to this shit, okay?"

"You don't like it, so go," Max said. "Take off, get your ass outta here."

"Yeah, like he says," Arnie added.

Pete stared at the two. "You jerkoffs in charge now, you runnin' the store? I oughta tell Rhino he don't have to come in, you guys don't need him no more."

Arnie frowned. "Mr. Schmitz hears you callin' him. . . what you said, *you* ain't going to be here no more."

"Yeah, right," Max said.

"Jesus, you guys make me sick." Peter scratched his crotch. "I ain't scared of *Rhino* Schmitz or anybody else, okay? Isn't no one in this whole goddamn town can tell – *whuuuh*?"

Pete went rigid as the front door of the office disappeared. A shower of broken glass filled the air. Max yelled and covered his eyes. Arnie grabbed the table, spilling cards and whiskey on his head.

The three men looked alike – black boots, black suits, black helmets on their heads. They stood a foot apart and opened fire. The weapons they carried were the new Congressional Ripper-Threes, sixteen-barrel Gattlings, seventy-two cal. One was enough to gut an entire parade. Three turned the tiny office into an instant slaughterhouse. In a quarter of a second, thirty-seven rounds sliced Pete in two. The top half looked surprised. The bottom half walked another step and then collapsed.

Max ran frantically for the back room. He almost made it; he was only half an hour slow. Arnie hid under the table. No one could find him there. Eighty-six copperheads splintered the wood and stitched him to the floor.

Colonel Victor Pryzer tossed the shattered door aside and stepped into the room. The office was thick with acrid smoke. Plaster and shredded cards drifted like confetti to the floor.

Chief Willis peered past Pryzer. His stomach lurched up into his throat. "My God, colonel. I don't know how you do things in D.C., but we do try to make an arrest now and then."

"Shit!" Pryzer slapped the nearest trooper in the

face. "What's the matter with you, sergeant? How the *hell* am I supposed to interrogate this mess?"

"Sir, sorry, sir!" The sergeant snapped to attention. "The suspects resisted, *sir*."

"Yeah, right." Pryzer nudged something red with his boot and made a face. "Any of these body parts belong to that Schmitz fella?"

"No. They just worked for him." Willis walked over to a shattered desk, found a pencil and poked through the bloody papers with the tip. "Krebs' file, a couple of mug shots. At least we know Schmitz was involved."

"Good. That's a big help." Pryzer nodded at his sergeant. "I'll want one of these bodies. Preferably one's still got a head." He turned and frowned at Willis. "This place is a goddamn dump. I thought those bail-bond jokers made a lot of dough?"

"They do," Willis said. "You've been in Steel Harbor a day now. What would you buy here?"

"Yeah, good point," Pryzer said.

Seventeen

It was two in the morning, high noon in hell. The far horizon glowed with a terrible light as Congressional forces dropped a thousand artillery shells in a minute on to the weakened Resistance lines. Barbara Kopetski drew in a breath and squeezed Axel's hand. God, the front was nearly twenty miles away and she could feel the thunder in the earth, feel the tremble in her belly.

"How could anyone live through that?" she said. "There can't be anyone left up there . . . there *can't* . . ."

"People are real stubborn," Axel said, "they don't like to die. They crawl out of the goddamn mud and count their arms and legs. Then they get up and fight again."

"Why would you *want* to be alive? I'd be mad as hell if I lived through that and knew I had to do it again."

For a moment, Axel didn't answer. He looked at the dark lines of troopers, the trucks whining and sliding over the muddy road. The road led to the front, to the killing fields where the shells were falling now.

"That's *their* war," he told her, "this one's ours."

"That's a pretty cynical way to look at it, pal."

Axel shook his head. "None of this is going to do a

105

damn bit of good. Even the poor bastards moving up there know that. This time tomorrow the Congressionals will roll right over them. The morning after that they'll be here."

He slipped his arm about her waist, turned her face up to his and touched her cheek.

"They'll pull the entire Resistance force out of Seattle before Racker's tanks get into the city. Promise me you and Charlie'll be on a chopper, all right? Don't do something dumb."

"Who, me?" Barbara laughed and slid her arms around his neck.

"Not funny. I mean it. I'm not losing you now."

"We'll be there," she assured him. "I'm worried about *you*."

"Nothing's going to happen to me. I've been on a million of these operations. Mop and mow, shoot and go. I'll see you at the choppers."

"You'd better."

The hard planes of his face were lit by the distant flashes of battle. She wanted to cry, but she knew she couldn't let him see that.

"When it's over, when we're out of this . . . then it's you and me. You want that, don't you?"

"You have to ask?" He showed her a lazy smile. "I thought you were a real bright lady –"

She cut off his words, with a finger to his lips. "*Don't*. Don't make jokes, not now."

"No jokes."

"Forever, Axel? I mean that. Just the way it sounds."

"Forever. And whatever comes after that."

She came to him, then, pressed herself close against

106

him, kissed him hard, kissed him with a hunger she didn't try to hide. She wanted him to know, wanted him to see she would never hold anything back, that there was only one way with her, and that was giving all she had, taking all he had to give.

They stood there a long moment, then he led her back into the dense stand of trees where the others were camped. He could smell the strong scent of coffee, hear them talking, telling jokes, cleaning their weapons for the next day's fight. They all knew what was coming, that many of them would likely never see another night, but that didn't stop their laughter now.

They stopped beneath the big, familiar oak, and sank to the thick bed of ferns, still holding each other close. Axel watched, didn't take his eyes off her as she quickly worked the buttons of her jacket, let it fall from her shoulders to the ground. She smiled as he reached for her, hooking his fingers in the tops of her camou trousers, sliding them down her legs.

She was on him, then, tearing at his clothes, her lips pressed to his face, covering him with kisses, whispering desperately in his ear, telling him everything she had never told him before. This time she couldn't hold back the tears and didn't try, and the tears moved from sadness to wonder to unrestrained joy, and, finally, remembering tomorrow, down the scale to sorrow once more . . .

She could hear the angry growl of the tanks rumbling like great, sluggish monsters through the streets not far away. As Axel had predicted, the American army had folded under the onslaught of the Congressionals, folded and run and clogged the roads with their dead and dying while their rearguard fought a desperate, suicidal battle to buy their companions time.

Now time had run out, and the American units still intact were pouring out of the south edge of the city, General Racker's bloody panzers on their heels. One tank division raced after them down Highway 5, through the embattled heart of Seattle, while another sped southwest in a pincer movement past Maple Valley toward Auburn. If the Americans could reach Tacoma and hold the lines . . .

Barbara shook her head. They'd never make it that far. If the tanks didn't get them on the ground, the endless waves of Leopard jets would get them from the air. As she watched, six of the tri-winged fighters screamed out of the north, dropped their wobbly loads and ripped black arcs across the sky.

Seconds later, yellow blossoms of napalm rose beyond the buildings to her right – far enough to miss the ragged screams, close enough to feel the heat.

"Damn you – *damn* you, you bloody bastards!" Barbara cried out. "Damn every –"

The earth shook as a shell struck half a block away. Barbara staggered, covering her face and fell.

Charlie yelled, coming at her in a broken run across the empty lot.

"You all right? Barbara? *Barbara*!"

He turned her over roughly, his heart in his throat. Relief turned to anger as she moaned and sat up.

"What the hell do you think you're doing out here? You going to stop a tank with *that*?" He nodded at her sidearm, a stocky Peruvian 9mm 'Gato'. "For Christ's sake, Barb, you can come back and play tourist when the war's over."

108

"I am *not* playing tourist, Charlie." She gave him a nasty look. "I'm a forward observer. I'm observing, okay?"

"Fine. Only –" Another shell chopped off his words. "Only, we don't *have* a forward anymore. All we've got's reverse. We're shuckin' this mother now. Pronto. Outta here."

Barbara stared at him, looked back the way he'd come. "Where's Axel? He's not here. I don't go without Axel."

"Axel said he'd be here, he'll be here."

"Yeah, well he's not. And if he's not, then I'm –"

"Damn it, sis, shut up and get out of here!"

Charlie grabbed her arm and ran. Three shells whined over the field in a straight, geometrically perfect line. Charlie cursed and threw both of them in a hole. The fourth and fifth explosions blew a ton of black earth into the air. Barb felt dirt rain down on her head. Something warm trickled on her cheeks, and she knew the blood was coming from her ears.

Charlie got them to their feet, heading down Jackson for the burned-out shell that used to be Union Station. Above the din of the shells they could hear the flat clatter of the choppers coming in. Barbara looked up and saw their dark, dragonfly silhouettes against the smoked-filled sky. The Congressional saw them too, stopped lobbing shells at the Resistance stronghold and turned their deadly Maxis straight up. The guns stuttered and filled the air with dirty balls of black. Barb gasped, stopped and brought her hand to her mouth as one of the choppers hit a fiery, invisible wall.

"Come on," Charlie yelled, "go-go-go!"

She followed him through the ruins of the terminal to the open space on the other side. Five of the choppers had made it in. Their rotors whirred as the Resistance fighters dragged themselves and their wounded toward the open doors.

Now the tanks turned back to their targets on the ground. Shells burst across the field. One chopper, loaded with men, turned into a ball of flame. Another blast tore a dozen running men to bloody shreds.

Charlie climbed into the nearest chopper, dropped his weapon and reached down to help his sister. Barb jerked back, pushing him away.

"Get *in*," Charlie told her. "Get in, Barb, do it now!"

"He'll be here," Barb said. "He said he'd be here, Charlie. I'm not going anywhere . . ."

Half a dozen forms staggered through the smoke. One fell and didn't get up. His buddy bent, looked at him, left him and ran for the chopper. Two soldiers passed her and pulled themselves aboard. Their faces were covered with grime, their eyes were red with weariness and fear. Barb squinted through the smoke. Charlie shouted at her, but Barb didn't hear. Three soldiers appeared, two dragging another between them. One of the men looked right at her.

"You're Barbara Kopetski, right?"

"Yes, yes! I *know* you –"

"Axel's still back there. He's not coming. He said: tell you he's sorry."

"What?" Barb grabbed the man's arm. "What does that mean, is he –"

The man pried her fingers away. "He can't come," he said, almost gently, "we didn't have time to talk about it, okay? Look, I'm sorry . . ."

Barb turned away, started walking from the choppers. Charlie knew his sister well, knew what he had to do. He jumped from the door, brought her down with a tackle that drove all the air from her lungs, picked her up and tossed her roughly into the chopper. Two of the men caught her, held her there screaming and beating at them with her fists. The chopper whined and lifted off the ground. Charlie muttered under his breath and leaped for the doorway. Hands grabbed him and pulled him aboard.

She cursed him, called him every name in the book, made up a few no one had ever heard before. He wouldn't look at her, he stayed at the door and kept his eyes on the ground. The choppers were only seconds ahead of the tanks. They broke through the rubble, raking the ground with their 98s, firing blindly through the smoke at anything left on the ground.

Charlie noted they were coming from the west now, instead of the north, from the direction of Elliot Bay. Maybe the column had split farther north on Highway 5, near the center of town. Maybe this bunch had crossed over and rumbled down the Alaskan Freeway.

And what the hell difference did it make where they'd come from, if they's swum up Puget Sound? The poor bastards down there didn't care . . .

Eighteen

She liked to be there by herself. Walk through the place when the bright lights were off and the glow from the street cast shadows on the floor.

Curly wouldn't do it. Curly got out of there fast when everyone was gone. Empty places didn't stay empty long, Curly said. Something came in to fill them up, and you didn't want to be there when it did.

Barb laughed at that. She told him the Hammerhead wasn't old enough to have ghosts. A new place was like soda-pop wine to a ghost; it didn't taste right, it didn't have a lot of class . . .

Yeah, well, Curly said, if class was a part of the deal, there wouldn't be a lot of places haunted at all, and, though he hated to say it, that included the Hammerhead.

Barb saw phantoms in the Hammerhead at night but not the ghostly kind. There were faces from the past, people she remembered, people who didn't have a name. Sometimes there was laughter, a few bars of a song. And maybe, she decided, some of the phantoms that came to her were ghosts after all. People from *that* past were more likely dead than alive.

Barb tried not to see them, tried not to hear the laughter, tried not to hear the songs. She didn't come to the empty dance floor, to the dark and lonely bar to stir memories of the past. She came downstairs in

the small gray hours because it was far less frightening to face the things she saw awake than the ones
who came to her in her sleep . . .

The cognac tasted good.

She rolled it around in the snifter, inhaled the heady
fumes. It was a Courvoisier, VSOP, mid-twentieth
century, incredibly smooth and rarer than rare.

A sad state of affairs, Barb thought. She might be
sitting in the dark, drinking the only bottle of its kind
left in the world. So many things were gone – used up,
wasted and destroyed – tastes, smells and delights no
one would ever know again.

*God, I've got to stop this. I'm getting more morose
than Charlie. Before you know it I'll be –*

Barb turned, twisted off the barstool, bent in a
crouch. The pistol was a blur in her hand, aimed
straight at the figure in the dark.

"Come out of there. *Now*, or you're dead!"

"There is no need for that. Really, Barb. I assure
you I mean no harm."

Barb stared. At first, she couldn't put the body to
the voice. Rhino Schmitz, all right, but the massive
shadow wasn't familiar at all.

"I don't think I've seen you standing up. I never
thought about you tall."

Schmitz cleared his throat. "A person of my . . .
dimensions . . . does not make a habit of remaining
upright any more than is absolutely necessary. It ruins
the whole day."

"Schmitz, what do you want? And how the hell did
you get in here in the first place?"

"I have a facility with locks and alarms. In my

113

youth, if you can believe it, I was rather slim and agile. I, ah, sometimes worked outside the law."

"Oh, yeah?" Barb set her weapon on the bar and sipped her drink. "As opposed to what you do now?"

Schmitz let out an enormous sigh. "Say what you will. I am beyond insults of any kind. I need to talk to you, Barb. I felt it was possible you might not let me in if I appeared during . . . normal working hours."

"You'd be right, too." She squinted at Schmitz. Wondered again if she was truly facing only one man instead of three. "Why would I want to talk to you? You screwed me out of a million bucks. I ought to blow your head off right now."

"A million is pocket change, Miss Wire, compared to what's going down." He spread his stubby hands. "I need your help. All I ask is that you listen to me. Please."

"Get in line," Barb said.

He caught sight of the bottle, read the label and rolled his eyes. "I'm awfully dry. Do you suppose I could have a glass of that?"

"No. Get out of here. I wouldn't give you a drink if your pants were on fire, Rhino."

Schmitz flinched at the name. "Barb, no one else can handle this. You still have connections. Everyone knows that."

"Everyone knows I'm neutral."

Schmitz beamed. "I know. You don't pick sides. That's the beautiful part of it, you see. You can deal with *every*body, that's why I came to you."

He stopped, wiped his brow with an oversized bandanna. Long speeches wore him out, and he'd been standing on his feet for some time.

"I can't go *anywhere*. The Congressionals broke into my office. My God, they killed everyone – slaughtered them. Now they're looking for me. I'm a dead man, Miss Wire."

"Aw . . ." Barb gave him a sorrowful smile. "I'll bet they don't want to pay you that million bucks for Krebs, huh? Poor ol' Rhino . . ."

"It isn't about Krebs anymore. It's about retinal contact lenses."

Schmitz hesitated, but Barb's expression didn't change. He brought a small, flat metal box from one of his voluminous pockets, set it in front of Barb, and carefully lifted the lid.

Barb leaned in close. A pair of blue contact lenses floated in a clear liquid.

"Sorry," Barb said. "Don't use 'em. I can see just fine."

Schmitz ignored her. "These were smuggled in from Germany. *Anyone* can place them over their eyes and pass through every retinal scanner ever made. Congressional, UN – doesn't matter. They cannot be detected."

"A very marketable item, I'd imagine."

Schmitz looked away. "I was going to sell them, yes. But my, ah, buyer, fell through at the last minute . . ."

"God, you're something else. When was the last time you told *yourself* the truth, Schmitz?" Barb shook her head. "Krebs is Resistance. Which means those lenses belong to his friends. You want to do yourself a favor, give 'em back. Say you're sorry."

Schmitz blinked. "Are you serious? They'd kill me!"

"Yeah, so?"

Schmitz brought out his bandanna again. Barb took a deep whiff of her cognac. The smell of the man's fear was enough to gag a goat.

"I know I double-crossed you. I deeply regret that now."

"Uh-huh. I'll bet."

"I do. Believe me. I made a big mistake. I'm willing to admit it, all right? I would like to make it up you now. I want to trade the lenses, I want you to have them."

Barb frowned. "What for?"

"A very small favor, an act of kindness on your part . . ."

"Don't push your luck," Barb said.

"Get me out of Steel Harbor. That's all. Get me out of here and they're yours."

"Forget it, Schmitz."

"*Forget it*!" Schmitz's whole body seemed to tremble, an awesome sight to see. "We are talking about my *life*, Barb! Please: tell me what to do, who to see. For Christ's sake, do that much and I'll *give* them to you!"

Schmitz staggered, caught himself and clutched at the bar. "Do you – do you have any idea what these are worth? You could get two million, Canadian. No, very likely more than that. Once the word gets out they're available –" A sudden thought struck him. "There's enough money in these lenses to get you to Europe. You could – you could get one of those neuro-electronic operations for Charlie's eyes. The things they can do these days. Marvelous advances, marvelous!"

116

"Get out. Get out of my sight right now."

"Uh, what?" Schmitz stared. Her eyes were in shadow, but he couldn't miss the ice in her voice. "You don't mean that. You wouldn't pass up a chance like this."

"Try me." Barb said. She picked up the metal box and tossed it at Schmitz. Schmitz caught it frantically and hugged it to his chest.

"You'll – you'll regret not helping me. You'll be very sorry for this . . ."

"Right. I'll put it on my list."

Barb turned her back on him, picked up the bottle and poured herself a drink. Schmitz backed off, making his way through the maze of tables and chairs. He paused, once, for a second and a half, took one last look at Barb and hurried through the kitchen to the back alley door.

Charlie heard him go.

When Charlie stood perfectly still he could hear things no one else could hear. Oddly enough, it didn't much matter if Charlie was sober or drunk. If anything, he felt his senses were far more acute when he was floating in alcohol. This may or may not have been true, but Charlie believed it was so.

He heard Barb's bottle click lightly against her glass, heard the dark liquid trickle down her throat. He heard Schmitz walk across the floor, heard his labored breathing, heard the worn boards groan beneath his weight. He heard Schmitz pause, heard the slight, almost imperceptible sound after that. Heard it, and smiled, because now Charlie knew something no one else could even guess. A blind man

117

knows a lot of things no else knows, and Charlie
Kopetski liked that . . .

A lot of really weird shit happens, you're right in the middle of it, you know? A guy, some guy you maybe know a long time, you don't even know the guy's name, something happens, you remember this guy, you won't ever forget him anymore.

I didn't know him, I knew he was there because he was good at what he did, which was killing Congressional sleaze, which is what we were trained for, right? I also remember him because he had a good-looking sister. I'm talking first class, I'm talking – okay, that don't matter, this ain't about her, that's not what it's about. What it is, see, we get out of Seattle after the big screw-up, a handful of Resistance guys holed up waitin' for the choppers, and the tanks are coming in blowing everything to hell. Finally, four or five choppers show up and we all pile in and two, maybe three make it out.

Anyway, I didn't see this guy again, a long time, then I see him again and his sister, too, we make a drop on the Montana border, some shithole right on the Little Bighorn River, and ain't that a crock, startin' another firefight there?

What we did, we dropped in on this firebase where the Congressionals had been before, we're waitin' for our supply drop, everybody says they're going to be droppin' beer, right? We're messin' around, just waiting for that, and we hear this kinda *whump!* and I'm saying, shit, man, I've heard that before.

We run over there and this guy's laying face down knocked out cold, and the medic turns him over and both his eyes are gone. He's stepped on a mine is what he's done, and Christ, all he's got are bloody holes, man. His sister is screaming and she won't let us give her a shot, and they take her away somewhere and that's that. Next day they lift us out and drop us in Utah which is also a lousy place to be. What I'm sayin' is, no one, no one's even scratched on this operation but this guy I'm talking about. Which is the kind of weird stuff that can happen in a war . . .

[Excerpt from *Memories of the Western Campaign*, C. R. Burrows, The Resistance Forces, Private Printing.]

– Johnny Gray Wolf, PhD, *Fall From Glory* (2032), University of the New Sioux Nation Press.

Nineteen

The place was a health club once. The walls had murals of happy nymphs and satyrs chasing each other through the woods. In the background there were temples in a vaguely Grecian style. Below the murals was an empty indoor pool. The bottom was cracked, and one side of the pool had caved in, leaving an avalanche of tiles.

At the deep end, black cables trailed over the edge like a tangle of lazy snakes. The cables were attached to a burnished steel machine. Three technicians in loose green coveralls hovered over a set of blinking dials. After a moment, one looked over his shoulder and nodded to a large man in black.

"We're all set here," he said. "You can go ahead, sir."

"About time, too." Colonel Victor Pryzer glared at the tech, then walked to the square concrete vat that sat just below an ancient diving board. The vat was lined with copper, and was filled to the top with water and chunks of ice.

Pryzer leaned over, dipped one finger in the cold water and quickly drew it out.

"We wastin' time, or you going to get something out of this mess? I *need* a goddamn answer, Doc."

"We'll get whatever he's got, Colonel. If it's there, fine. If it's not . . ."

The man let his words trail off. He was a short man with a gaunt, almost skeletal frame. His face was acne-scarred, and he'd tried to cover the problem with a beard. The beard grew in sparse irregular tufts and did very little good.

As Pryzer watched over his shoulder, Doc spat out his cigarette and plunged a heavy surgical glove into the freezing water. The remains of Arnie Welch, former card-player and one-time employee of Thomas "Rhino" Schmitz, rose to the surface. Bullets had ripped him apart, and most of his body was a ragged mix of flesh and bone. Nobody cared about his body, however; they cared about his head. His head was just fine, his head was still intact. It was clean-shaven now, and the bloodless scalp was punctured with a dozen colored wires.

"The subject is reasonably fresh," the Doc said, squeezing a pinch of blue skin, "but I can't promise more than a couple of seconds of reasonable thought data. Ah, cognitive impressions, so to speak. The closest to the moment of expiration, usually. After that, whatever snippets are left."

"Snippets," Pryzer said, raising a brow at the doctor. He didn't care for people who used words like that. 'Snippet' didn't sound very serious, and it certainly wasn't military at all. Your average science bigdome type thought he was too good for anybody else. Especially soldiers – men who got out in the field and died instead of fooling around in an air-conditioned lab.

Maybe he'd hook this one up in a tub of ice water sometime, Pryzer thought. See what was in *his* friggin' head.

"I'm not promising snippets, you understand. Sometimes all you get is neural soup. Shattered memories. Bit and pieces of dreams. Whatever. Don't expect a cable special, Colonel. Medically speaking, the stuff this bozo's got left is likely pretty raw shit."

"Record it," Pryzer said. "Everything. Whatever's in there I want it."

"Yes, sir."

The young officer behind the colonel switched on a small device. It was the same device – an analyzer with a monitor screen attached – that Pryzer had used in the abandoned auto parts shop. The same silver wires now ran from the head of Arnie Welch to the machine.

"Clear," said the officer; "we're hot and on line."

The doctor nodded. The deep throb of energy echoed throughout the big room. The vat of ice water crackled with half a million volts. The corpse twitched and writhed as if it might escape this torture somehow. A thousand images blurred across the monitor screen. Smoke rose from the vat, and the unpleasant odor of fried Arnie Welch filled the air.

Finally, the machinery whined down, ground to a halt and died. Colonel Pryzer squinted at the screen, then frowned at the doctor.

"That's it, that's all you got?"

"No, Colonel," the doctor said patiently, "that is *not* all. That is real-time remembrance you see on the screen. Compressed thought patterns. Everything squeezed together in small parts of a second. Much too fast to read. We have to play it back in slow motion." Doc gave Pryzer a patronizing smile. "The thought, you see, is quicker than the eye."

123

Keep talking, you son of a bitch. I'm taking names and yours is at the top of the list . . .

Doc conferred with the officer who sat before the monitor device, gave a few suggestions and stepped away. The officer began to tap a rapid code. The screen began to quiver, tremble and ripple like water disturbed on the surface of a dark and bottomless lake . . .

From the start, Chief Willis had kept his distance, stayed well out of the way. The bloodbath in Rhino Schmitz's office was disgusting in the extreme, but he'd seen people shot up before. It was something that went with the job, and a cop got used to that. Pale white corpses floating in ice water, that was a bit too much.

Still, when the twitching and the bubbling was over, he walked up behind the others and watched the monitor screen. People parts were one thing, peering into somebody's head was something else. He told himself it was strictly professional interest, but he knew, in his heart, that the idea had a pleasantly kinky appeal

The monitor showed a hand of cards . . . three hearts, a club and something else . . . the cards blinked, disappeared . . . A man's face swam on to the screen, then another . . . the other man had cards too . . . The images vanished again . . . A man in black fired directly at Arnie's chest . . . he saw the man's eyes half a second before he fired, knew he liked to kill, this is what he liked to do . . .

. . . a brilliant flash of red . . . static . . . nothing . . . static again . . .

... *Krebs, William Krebs ... he was tied to a chair, staring straight at the screen ... his mouth open in a long and silent scream ... he could see the needle-nose pliers in Arnie's hand, could see them coming closer to his eyes, knew what Arnie was going to do ...*

... *static ... nothing ... static again ...*

... *pages of a porno magazine flickered by ... splinters of an unlikely dream ...*

... *a car ... a home ... a memory twenty years old ... then a sudden flash ... Barb Wire, her pistol pressed against Krebs' head ... Barb disappears ... a white dog runs across a field ... a child in a blue dress laughs ... chocolate ice cream ...*

... *static ... nothing ... the screen goes black ...*

"By God ..." Pryzer slammed a big fist into his palm. "By God, I've got her now."

He jerked around to face Willis. "Issue a warrant for the arrest of Barb Wire. I want her in custody an hour ago!"

Willis frowned. "Colonel, this isn't Washington! I need a reason to make an arrest."

Pryzer stared. "*Citizen* Barb Wire is involved in a case involving national security. That's all the reason you need. Do it."

"You're basing all this on that very short image of her, right? Your doctor said sometimes all you get are dreams. In Steel Harbor everybody dreams about Barb Wire. Some sleazo's fantasy mixed up with a face that might be William Krebs ... that won't cut it. You'll have to do better than that."

Pryzer looked pained. "When did the rules ever

125

bother you, *Chief*? I know how you make your living in this town. That's why you're here."

"I don't – always walk a fine line, all right? But I walk *my* line, Colonel."

"Oh, Great Jesus . . ." Pryzer rolled his eyes. He showed Willis a disarming smile, took a step forward and drew Willis aside.

The smile disappeared. "Listen, mister, you got no business knowin' this, but if you're going to have a friggin' moral attack – : your Miss Wire is in this mess over her head. She's mixed up with Krebs, and that means she's probably got something I need."

"Like what?"

"A pair of – a pair of contact lenses. Retinal contact lenses."

"That's what this is all about? Contact lenses?"

"No, goddamn it, it's about bringing in an enemy of the Congressional Republic, a traitor named Cora D.!"

Willis look bewildered. Pryzer muttered to himself.

"I'm sayin' this once," he told Willis. "*You* don't say it to anyone else. These aren't ordinary lenses. There's nothing like 'em anywhere. This Cora D. is going to try to use them to get past the UN scanners in the freeport and get on a plane to Canada."

Pryzer poked a finger in Willis's chest. "If Cora D. gets out of Steel Harbor it's going to be embarrassing to the Republic. It's going to be *real* embarrassin' to me. And if it's embarrassin' to me, it is going to be *painfully* embarrassing to you, Willis. Do you understand, do you read me, mister?"

Willis felt his throat go dry. "I think I . . . understand your feelings on this."

126

"Sir."

"Sir. Yes, sir. What I can do, I can –"

"What you can do is what I tol' you to do, Chief. And right now that'd be issuing a search warrant for the Hammerhead."

Willis looked past Pryzer. One of the colonel's black-clad goons had stuck a cigar in the corpse's mouth. The goons, the doctor, everyone on hand was doubling up in laughter. Willis felt his lunch coming up and swallowed hard.

"I can handle that," he said. "I'll get on it right away."

"Good, good." Pryzer showed a mouthful of teeth. "I love it when everything's runnin' real smooth, don't you?"

Twenty

The tub was an antique jacuzzi. It was made of real Italian marble instead of fiberglass. At one time, many years before, it had graced the hideaway of the governor of a large eastern state. The governor's assorted playmates had cavorted in the tub, where they scrubbed the governor's back and performed various other services the governor liked a lot. The governor and his companions were long dead, and his state was a deep crater lake. The jacuzzi, though, was still intact. It belonged to Barb Wire, and had been smuggled into Steel Harbor at no small expense.

Barb allowed herself few idle hours and even fewer frills. Her motorcycles, scarce cognac and the price-less marble tub were at the top of a very short list. Somewhere up there were comfortable, soft-hide leather boots, firearms that worked and imported shampoo.

The jets of water massaged every lovely inch, rippled along her perfect flesh, drained the last hint of tension from her body and her mind and left her pleasantly limp. The shampoo buried her in a frothy white cloud. Only her face and the tips of her breasts betrayed her presence in the tub.

The smart thing to do, she told herself – not for the first time, of course – was to sell out now, take the money and run. New offers came in every day, offers so fat they made her want to cry. Nobody knew for sure what she was hauling in at the Hammerhead, but they could count the traffic in the place and they had a good idea.

Do it now, Curly said, while you've still got the chance . . . the war won't last forever, and when it's over this place'll be as popular as the city dump . . .

He was right, too, Barb knew. Steel Harbor was a unique haven in a country torn by civil war. And, while the Hammerhead Bar & Grill wasn't the only spot in town, it was the only one that counted. And when the war was over and done . . .

When the war was over and done, she told herself, you couldn't *give* the place away . . .

Barb let out a breath. So sell out now – and do what? Rhino Schmitz said Europe, and of course she'd considered it before. That was mostly bullshit about fixing Charlie's eyes, though – nothing could do that.

He could drink cheap there, there's that . . . but what would I do? Open up another place? La Barb's Parisian Rendezvous?

She laughed aloud at that, an unlikely picture form-ing in her head – a place that looked half like the Hammerhead and half like a place that would attract a little guy named Lautrec.

Reaching for a sponge, she wiped the foam from her eyes and picked up the snifter of cognac on the edge of the jacuzzi. *Why did it always taste better in a steaming tub of water? Maybe for the same reason the heat of your hand enhanced the liquid in the gl –*

Barb stopped, the snifter halfway to her lips. The glass panel surrounding the tub was fogged with steam. She stared as the message began to appear:

D-O-N-T

S-H-O-O-T

Barb cursed under her breath, grabbed the Peruvian automatic from behind her shampoo and aimed the weapon squarely at the glass. A hand wiped away a circle of fog. The words vanished, and Axel's face appeared.

"Easy," he said, "I'm unarmed. You don't want to shoot an unarmed man."

"Not ordinarily," Barb said between her teeth, "but I'm willing to make an exception."

Axel showed her a stupid grin and spread his jacket wide. *See?* his gesture said: *no rockets, no grenades – no Ranger knives.*

Barb stood and slid the glass aside. The pistol didn't waver from Axel's head.

"Are you crazy? How the hell did you get in here, anyway? Where's my dog?"

Axel's mouth dropped open. He thought he'd remembered how she looked, but the memories weren't nearly as vivid, as shapely or as naked as Barb herself; Barb tall and slender, her skin slick and fine, clothed in a million tiny bubbles that were quickly disappearing before his eyes.

"Stop that," she said. "You look like a ten-year-old kid. Get me a towel."

There were stacks of towels on hand, but Axel took his time. There were white towels and blue towels, pink towels and –

"Damn you, quit foolin' around." She stepped out

of the tub, grabbed a towel from his hand and wrapped it around herself.

"Now. You didn't answer my question. How'd you get in here, and where's my dog?"

"That's two questions."

"Axel . . ." She aimed the pistol at his belly.

"Okay, all right. I broke in. You've got lousy locks. Your dog's right here."

Barb squinted through the steamy air. Camille was lying with her head at Axel's feet.

"What can I say? I'm irresistible to women."

"No, you're not. Camille's a bitch. What do you want here, Axel? I told you never to come back."

"You going to shoot me with that?"

"Shit . . ." She tossed the gun in the sink, swept past him through her bedroom and up the stairs.

"I came to Steel Harbor to do a job, Barb. The biggest operation I ever signed on for. I was ready for anything the Congressionals could throw at me. The only thing I wasn't ready for was – running into you."

"You'll get over it. I did."

"Barb, listen to me, damn it!"

"I did. Remember? I listened to everything you said, every promise you made. I want you out of here, Axel. Now."

She climbed the stairs to her office, Axel at her heels. She stopped, then turned on him and glared.

"I'll go when I'm through talking to you. You might as well calm down and listen, Barb . . ."

Barb drew in a breath. Her hand went to her side, but there was nothing there but a towel.

"You left your gun downstairs," Axel said. "I could wait, you want to go and get it."

"I've got plenty of guns," Barb muttered, "don't you worry about that." She stomped to her desk, started opening drawers and slamming them shut. "Damn it, where's a weapon when you need one!"

"I wouldn't have come here unless I had to. I think you know that."

"Well I sure as hell wouldn't *be* here if I'd known you were coming. You –" She stopped, looked at Camille. Camille was taking it all in, happily wagging her tail. "As for you –" Barb jabbed a finger at the dog. "You and I are going to have a long talk, lady."

Camille whined, lowered her head and slithered under the desk.

Barb gave up on the drawers and turned on Axel in disgust.

"How could you do it? How could you have the nerve to show up after all this time? How could you even thing that I'd – I'd –"

Axel reached out, gripped her shoulders and pulled her roughly to him. Barb opened her mouth to protest, looked in his eyes, then buried her hands in his hair and pressed her lips hard against his own.

Axel held her, his hands about her waist. Barb moaned, slid her arms around his neck, molded her body to his. He lifted her high, held her until her toes left the floor . . .

"Sorry, am I interrupting something?"

Barb brought her hand to Axel's chest and pushed him away. She stared at the woman, then turned on Axel.

"Just lovely. You brought company."

Axel let out a breath and stepped away. "Ah, Barb, this is – Cora D.. We've been working together."

"I'm sure you have." She gave Corrina a deadly sweet smile. "Axel does such good work. Everyone says so."

"Barb, you don't underst –"

"Oh, for God's sake, Axel. If you try to *explain* anything to me I'll throw up."

"All I wanted in Seattle was to disappear with you and never look back. The war got in the way. The war . . . changed that. It changed everything."

Barb raised a brow. "Yeah? I hadn't heard."

Axel looked miserable. He glanced at Corrina, saw no help there and looked at the floor. "Okay. I'm not surprised you don't believe me. No reason you should. I knew you were waiting at the choppers and I knew I couldn't get back. Not without leaving undone what I had to do.

"By the time the mission was over we were completely cut off. We had to get back through the Congressional lines, up past the Skagit River across into British Columbia. It took us six months to get smuggled back into American occupied territory."

Barb ran her fingers through her hair. "You didn't think I'd wait for you? For six months?"

"It wasn't that, it was a lot of things."

"Fine. I'm listening. What kind of things?"

"Axel is not being entirely fair to himself," Corrina put in. "Some things got in his way. I'm one of those things, I guess."

Barb gave her a cold, appraising look from head to toe. "Axel's got good taste, no one's going to argue that. It's his *timing* that's so goddamn lousy. He can't remember who he's with and where he's supposed to be."

"No, you're not listening," Corrina said. "The people who got him back through the lines are the same people who snapped him up for me. For *my* mission." Corrina looked straight at Barb. "I'm sure you know what happened in Topeka, Kansas. I don't think there's anyone who doesn't."

"Of course I do. The whole town went down the tubes. Some new – virus or something wiped out the entire population. No one's ever come up with an answer."

"I know the answer, Miss Wire."

Barb's eyes narrowed. "Uh-huh. And I'll bet you're going to tell me, too."

Corrina let out a breath. "My name isn't Cora D.. It's Corrina Devonshire. Dr. Corrina Devonshire. I – used to be the head of medical research for the Congressional Directorate . . ."

Barb started to speak. Corrina raised a hand to cut her off.

"I said *used* to be. I was not political at the time. Like you, I suppose. All I was interested in was my work.

"Then something happened to change all that. I discovered a secret project had been under way at our facility. Right under my nose. I would never have found out if they hadn't made a mistake. Certain . . . unusual formulae showed up on my computer. Things that weren't supposed to be there but obviously were."

Corrina leaned against Barb's desk. Recalling the past seemed to draw a dark shadow across her eyes, drain her of strength.

"I followed the paper trail. I – learned that some of my associates – people I trusted before – were work-

134

ing directly under someone high in the Congressional government. I learned that they had developed a biological weapon, an HIV derivative known as Red Ribbon. It's contagious as the common cold and it kills in twelve hours."

Corrina paused. "Topeka wasn't an accident, Miss Wire. It was a lab experiment. If it worked there – and we all know it did – then the Congressionals planned to unleash Red Ribbon against the Free Territories. I don't think I have to tell you what that would do."

"I expect it would get out of hand and kill *everybody*," Barb said. "Congressionals, Americans, cats, dogs – the whole country. Weapons have a way of doing that. They tend to get out of hand."

"That's about the size of it," Axel said. "The bastards never think of that."

"They found out I'd discovered their secret," Corrina said. "I got my hands on some of their material, then I managed to get in touch with the Resistance. Just in time, too. Half an hour later and I would've been dead." She looked at Axel. "They sent him in to get me out of Washington. The Congressionals didn't give up, of course. We've been on the run ever since."

Barb gave Axel a sour look. "That was goddamn heroic of you. maybe we can get you a medal."

"Hey, look – !" Axel's face colored.

"It's a terrific story. I'm impressed, and I'm not a bit surprised. Nothing *anyone* does in this war surprises me. Okay? So what am I supposed to do about it? What do you want out of me?"

"Your help, that's all," Axel said. "The cause needs your help if you'll give it."

135

Barb made a noise in her throat. "My, what a shocker. Someone wants my help." She gave Axel an icy look. "Just what the hell has the *cause* done for me lately?"

"Corrina has the formula for the antidote, Barb. She got away with that, which is why they're so eager to get her back. That and the fact she *knows* about Red Ribbon, of course."

"If we can get to Canada," Corrina put in, "I can tell the Truce Commission about Red Ribbon. That's the only way to stop the Congressionals. If the whole world knows what they're up to . . ."

"Good luck," Barb said, "hope you make it. Saving the world's a real nice thing to do."

"Damn it, Barb, what's the matter with you?" Axel stepped up to her. His eyes were on fire; the cords in his neck were taut with rage. "Don't you get it? This hasn't got anything to do with you and me. It's –"

Barb rolled her eyes. "Oh, please. The next line's 'This is bigger than both of us, Barb.' My God, somebody find me a violin."

Axel turned away. "Barb, the contact lenses. Where are they? We've got to have them. Right now."

"Huh?" Barb raised a brow. "Now where did *that* come from?"

"I'm asking you . . ."

"If I knew, you think I'd tell you?"

"Schmitz was here last night. We know that."

"Yeah, he was. And I threw him out. Do I have to write it on the wall for you people? I am not in this war anymore. I'm out, I'm neutral. One hundred percent."

Corrina closed her eyes. "If you know where he is,

if you know where those lenses are and won't tell us – for Christ's sake, Miss Wire, name – name a price. That's what you do, isn't it? Sell yourself to the highest bidder?"

"Corrina . . ." Axel warned.

"I am out of your price range, lady. You don't have the bucks to play in my league."

"If I don't have it I can try and get it."

"How? Pass the hat around the Resistance? That'll get you ten, twenty bucks. Forget it. Get out of here, leave Steel Harbor and disappear somewhere. The game you're playing is –"

Barb froze, jerked her head toward the stairs. She didn't have to ask – she'd heard the sound before. Wood shrieked and splintered and the front door of the Hammerhead slammed to the floor.

Barb turned to Axel and Corrina. "Wonderful. I have you two to thank for this. We've got *more* company now . . ."

Twenty-One

Charlie didn't spill a drop.

He calmly sipped his drink and set it on the bar. The noise of the front door exploding was obvious enough. You didn't need sensitive hearing for that. Still, Charlie Kopetski filtered other sounds from the assault upon his ears. The heavy boots stomping over wood and broken glass belonged to the Steel Harbor Police – six of them – and all but one had the standard metal rings on their heels.

There were other men, too. The one with the better quality boots and the stork-like stride was Chief Willis. The one that pounded the floor like a bull in heat was Colonel Pryzer.

"Do not seek justice or peace in this imperfect world," Charlie said to himself. "Who said that? Hell, maybe I did."

He heard and felt the cop coming at him, heard his labored breath, smelled his booze and sweat, smelled his leather belt. Smelled army-issue cigarettes, shaving soap and barley soup.

He flinched slightly as the cop jammed a portable retinal scanner in his face. The scanner gave a non-committal beep.

"Sir. No retinal scan available. I don't get no reading at all."

"Goddamn it." Willis grabbed the cop's arm and

jerked him away. "The man doesn't have any *eyes*. You don't have eyes, you don't have retinas either, you fool."

"Uh, sorry, sir." The cop dropped the scanner on the bar and trotted off. Willis looked at Charlie.

"Sorry about that. I'm recruiting from under rocks these days."

"I guess it's the war," Charlie said.

"Yeah, I guess it is. Where's Barb, you know, Charlie?"

"Am I my sister's keeper?"

Willis gave him a curious look.

Charlie grinned. "Now I *know* who said that . . ."

Barb peered through the blinds that covered her view of the main floor of the Hammerhead. Willis's goons were trashing the place with their usual gentle touch – smashing chairs, overturning tables, stealing bottles from the bar.

"You're getting the bill for this," Barb said. "You and *Doctor* Devonshire."

Axel looked over her shoulder. "They're not going to stay down there long. Is there another way out of this place?"

Barb muttered to herself. "God, I really needed this. Okay, I'll handle it. Stay put right there. Give me three minutes, then follow me down the stairs."

"Do what?"

Barb nailed Axel with her eyes. "No *whats*, pal – just do it."

She turned away before he could answer, walked quickly to the closet behind her desk. She dropped the towel, let it slip down her hips, down her thighs and to the floor.

Corrina drew in breath, stared at Barb Wire's perfect – and perfectly naked – shape before it was covered once more by a robe.

"Don't panic," Barb said without turning around, "I'm straight, lady. You're absolutely safe."

Axel repressed a grin. Corrina glared at him and he looked the other way.

"How do we know you won't turn us in to those people?" Corrina said. "Why should we trust you?"

"Maybe you shouldn't. Maybe you should open a window and fly out of here."

"Look, you've already told us you don't intend to help. If you – if you do plan to turn us in, I'd like to know that now."

Barb looked pained. "You going to swallow a poison pill or what?" She tightened her belt around her robe, opened the door and started down the stairs.

Willis looked up and spotted her at once. Pryzer scowled, then a smile creased his broad face.

"I'd strongly suggest you get yourself down here immediately, Miss Wire. The Congressional Republic has urgent business with you."

"Try me later," Barb said. "We're not open for breakfast."

Pryzer looked her over, thought about the delights that lay hidden beneath her robe. Fortune had a way of bringing pleasures his way, even pleasures as unlikely as Barb Wire.

"This is a perfectly legal entry, in case you intend to object. We have a warrant. Signed by a Steel Harbor judge. Willis –" Pryzer jerked a fat thumb over his shoulder. "Show her the warrant, Willis."

Willis gave Barb an apologetic shrug. Barb looked at the paper, took it from Willis in two fingers. She wrinkled her nose and dropped it to the floor.

"It's a little . . . sticky, Chief. What'd you do, carry it over here in your shorts?" She set her hands on her hips. "Okay, jokers, what the hell is this all about? You want to tell me or am I supposed to guess?"

"It's a murder investigation, Barb," Willis said patiently. "I don't have any choice but to carry out this warrant to the full extent of the law."

"What it is, is a top-priority, urgent and sensitive matter relating to the security of the Congressional Republic," Pryzer put in. He drew a deep breath and hitched up his pants. "I assure you, Citizen, that your complete cooperation is required. And I warn you that if I discover you are in any way involved in this affair the consequences to you will be both immediate and severe. Any attempt on your part to – huh?"

Pryzer stopped, blinked and looked curiously up the stairs. "Now who the hell are these people, what are they doing up there?" He jabbed his finger like a weapon. "You two. Get yourselves down here at once!"

Barb yawned. "Don't have a stroke, Colonel. They're mine."

"They're what?"

"Mine. Hired help. I picked them up on the boulevard. I like a good – *menage* now and then."

Pryzer closed one eye. "What's that? You talkin' American words or something else?"

"It means him, her and me, hon. Fun and games. Variations and thrills." Barb gave him a wink. "Ought to try it sometime."

"Huh," Pryzer said. He had a number of things in mind he'd like to try.

Barb opened the cash register at the bar, fingered out a stack of bills, slapped them in Axel's palm. "Go out by the kitchen. People tend to talk."

Axel took Corrina's arm and started across the floor.

"Hold it, just a minute," Willis said. He stepped in front of the pair, looked them up and down with his radar-cop eyes.

"I'm going to have to see your medical cards, people. Get 'em out."

"For God's sake," Barb moaned. "They're *streeties*, Willis, okay? They don't *have* medical cards. About half the people in Steel Harbor don't have cards, you know that."

Willis frowned. "Yeah, well . . ."

"Scan 'em," Pryzer said. He gave Willis a chilling look. "You are wastin' government time here, Chief. Let's get it moving, son."

Barb drew in a breath. She risked a look at Corrina. The woman's eyes widened a sixteenth of an inch. Unless you were looking right at her you couldn't tell. She's got guts, Barb thought, I'll give her that.

One of Willis's goons reached for the scanner on the bar, and moved toward Axel and Corrina. Axel's expression didn't change, but Barb saw his fingers move. When everything went bad, she knew he'd go for the weapon in his jacket, do what he had to do . . .

Corrina stared straight ahead. She could smell the cop's sour breath. The cop pressed the retinal scanner

142

to her face. It clicked like a locust on a hot summer night, made a high-pitched *ping*! and went quiet.

The goon brought the device up to the light. He tapped it with his fingers, shook it, tapped it again.

"I don' know, sir."

"What do you mean you don't know?" Willis said.

"It's broken, sir." He looked helplessly at his boss. "I can try an' fix it if you want."

"Goddamn it!" Pryzer ground a fist into his palm. "Your people are idiots, Willis. Wouldn't last five minutes in *my* army." He glared at Axel and Corrina. "Get out. Get out of here!"

Axel took Corrina's arm again and hurried toward the kitchen.

"Bye," Barb said, and gave the two a wave. "We'll do it again sometime." She turned on Pryzer. "Colonel, I've got a business to run. Is this going to take a long time?"

Pryzer looked as if he'd tasted something bad. "It is going to take as long as I want it to take, Citizen Wire. You got any strong objections to that?"

Barb turned to Charlie at the bar. "Get Franko and his crew on the phone, little brother. We're going to need some new furniture. And I want that *door* replaced before we open up again tonight. God, I don't suppose you people could just knock, wait for someone to let you in?"

Willis shook his head. "SLEP, Standard Law Enforcement Procedure, Barb. Wait around like that and your suspect's going to have time to hide shit of every sort, destroy evidence and get his hands on illegal firearms, which he might then use on official personnel."

"Uh-huh. And what if you bust into a place and don't find anything, what then?"

"Not a total loss. It's good training for the men." Willis grinned. "Hell, Barb, nobody's perfect. Not even your local police."

They sat at the bar. Barb poured herself a drink, reached for Charlie's glass and poured him one too. The place looked like a corps of Congressional tanks had passed through. Charlie had called the clean-up squad but they were late. Finally they called and said there'd been a major riot in the south end of town. Three UN soldiers were dead, nine wounded, four missing. No count on civilians yet, and traffic piled up for miles.

Barb looked at Charlie. "Man, this is awful. It wasn't this bad New Year's Eve. I wish you could see this mess."

"No big deal. I never saw it when it was clean." He sniffed his drink, took a deep slug and smacked his lips. "You got any idea what those clowns were looking for? They seemed to have something in mind."

"They did. I don't guess I told you. Rhino Schmitz dropped in last night. Uninvited, by the way. He's got these goddamn contact lenses. Wanted to trade 'em to me for a one-way ticket out of town. Seems he's got his enormous ass in a sling."

"Contact lenses."

"That's what I said."

"Ah, you mean like these?"

Charlie lifted his glasses. Stuck in the folds of scarred and puckered flesh were two bright blue circles of glass.

"Good God . . ." Barb was more stunned by the startling effect than by the fact that Charlie had the lenses. "What are you doing with those? How'd you get them from Schmitz?"

"I've got good ears," he said, "and Rhino makes a lot of noise."

Barb frowned. "You were in here? Last night?"

"Trade secret. I tell you and they'll kick my ass out of the Sacred Lodge of the Blind. I won't get to wear a funny hat anymore."

He took a flat metal carton from his pocket and dropped the lenses in. "I got to know. What color are they, Barb?"

"The color of money, Charlie. The color of lots and lots of money."

Charlie's smile faded. "Forget that. They're for Axel and the woman. These lenses are their way out of here."

"Huh-uh. They're out ticket to Europe, Charlie. Yours and mine."

Charlie grabbed for the metal box. Barb quickly slid it out of reach.

"No. They don't belong to us. We can't keep them."

"Watch me, pal."

"Damn it, Barb –"

She grabbed his hand and held it. "I know what's going on in that head of yours, so just drop it. We're neutral now. There are no sides in this war worth dying for. Look at you. What did you get out of the – out of the *cause*?"

"I'm not waving any flags," he told her. "I just think there are things that are right and things that aren't."

"Yeah, right. Well cheer up, baby brother. What's *right* is you and I are rich and we're getting out of this shithole for good."

She picked up the box and slipped it into the pocket of her robe. She looked curiously at Charlie, then turned and glanced at the door to the kitchen where Axel and Corrina had disappeared.

"If that scanner hadn't broken Pryzer would have strung up Axel and the woman by their heels. And you and me as well. That was an awful lucky break, seems to me."

"Yeah, well luck happens. Same as the other stuff." He emptied his glass and set it down. Reached two fingers in the pocket of his shirt and dropped a tiny frayed wire on the bar. "You leave your equipment lyin' around, it can go all to hell. Maintenance is the key."

Barb laughed. "Those tricky hands of yours, brother. I should've known." She kissed Charlie on the cheek, slipped off the bar stool and started for the stairs.

"Barb . . ."

She stopped. Charlie didn't look up. He wrapped one hand around his empty glass. "This isn't right. You're – making a mistake doing this. A real big one this time."

Barb bit her lips. She tried to remember him, how he'd been before. It worried her that she couldn't recall how Charlie had looked with eyes. The picture simply wasn't there.

"Tell me that again when we get to Paris," she said.

146

My heart is indeed heavy as I address the American people tonight. For some time now, my fellow Congressmen and I, your voices in Washington, your elected representatives, have labored long and hard to find a reasonable solution to the many problems that have plagued our great nation these many, many years. We have watched this administration, and the one before it, bring the economy, the health, the very moral fiber of our country to the brink of chaos. We have done everything within the limits of our legislative powers to convince the President that we were on a path that could lead to nowhere but disaster.

Now, to preserve the freedom of the American people, we have been forced to make a most painful and agonizing decision. At this moment, as I speak to you, the President, his Cabinet, and all those who serve him have been arrested by Special Forces of the newly formed Army of the Congressional Republic. These same forces are now joined in battle with a number of units of the rebellious United States Armed Forces who have refused to pledge their loyalty to the Congressional Flag.

Let me assure you, my fellow citizens, that this civil disturbance will be brief, that peace and order will be restored as quickly and as painlessly as possible. The American Republic is, of course, in no danger whatever. Rumors of actual attacks on

American cities are completely false – fright tactics initiated by those who would thwart the peaceful and democratic aims of the new Congressional Republic.

As citizens, you can do your part to help bring about the country's return to normalcy by simply following the temporary rules that have been instituted for your safety. These rules will soon be available in your local newspaper and on television, but I will go over them briefly here:

- Obey the curfew hours. Emergency conditions often encourage criminal elements to take advantage of peaceful citizens.
- Do not gather in groups of more than four. While Congressional military forces will take every precaution to avoid misunderstandings, the presence of large groups must necessarily be regarded as potential treasonable activity.
- Do not leave the city limits of your present home address without specific permission from civil or military authorities. It is anticipated that "pro-Presidential" troops and misguided "Resistance" forces will attempt to infiltrate and/or leave urban areas for the purpose of disruptive actions.
- Do not utilize restricted radio or TV channels. Civil insurrectionists will

attempt to use the media to misinform the public.

- Do not use your telephone except in life and death emergencies.
- Do not attend religious services, civic gatherings, lodge or fraternal meetings, etc., until further notice.
- Turn in all firearms at once to local police units.
- Study the list of harmful and misleading books, newspapers, magazines, works of fiction, misleading historical documents, etc.. A list of such materials will be posted shortly in all public places.
- Some individuals – even friends, neighbors or family members – may seek to undermine the Congressional Republic. As a citizen, it is your duty to inform local authorities of these persons.
- You may obtain the new Congressional flags, and the Congressional armbands, from the Congressional Party headquarters that will soon open in your neighborhood. Persons in authority there will also be glad to introduce you to the new Congressional salute. You are encouraged to show your support for the Congressional Republic by utilizing the flag, armband and salute on all appropriate occasions.

Briefly, my friends these are a few of the rules and regulations that will aid you in helping your newly formed government bring about a quick return to the free, productive and more meaningful lives denied you under the corrupt administrations of the past several decades. Again, I want to assure you that the reins of government will pass smoothly from the old to the new, with little interruption or discomfort to you, the citizens of this nation.

God bless you, and God bless the New Congressional Republic . . .

[Excerpt from the address of the Speaker of the House, on the eve of the founding of the Congressional Republic.]

– Johnny Gray Wolf, PhD, *Fall From Glory* (2032),
University of the New Sioux Nation Press.

Twenty-two

Steel Harbor hid a thousand sins by night. Darkness masked hunger, hatred and regret, ugliness and death. Bad wasn't half-bad at all, and a lie as lovely as the truth.

Dawn caught the city naked and ashamed, every secret, every sordid act revealed. The people of the night, the Snakers and the Scanners, the Skinners and the Slicks were back in their hidey-holes, safe from the morning, safe from the unforgiving light.

Now the denizens of the day could appear. The Stompers began to make their rounds, catching hapless traders unaware, taking half their goods, giving them a hit or two and sending them on their way. No one robbed a trader blind; a trader would come back another day.

Just after first light the first of the children appeared, big eyes and bloated bellies, sticks for arms and legs. The Grabbers liked to wait, wait until the children got the best of the garbage, the cream of the scraps – then they would jump the packs hard, rip 'em of and run.

The children were hungry, but the children weren't dumb. Soon the Grabbers started feeling real bad, started screaming and writing and wishing they were dead – and some of them were, at that.

Must've been something they ate, the children said;

what a dirty shame, they said. And that was all there was to that . . .

Big Fatso liked the morning. Big Fatso liked the sun. He liked to get naked and lie on the hood of a '99 Caddy and watch himself sweat. Big Fatso naked was an awesome thing to see. Weighing in at seven-oh-three, he made Rhino Schmitz look like the poster boy for Anorexic Week.

The sun was veiled by a poison cloud that hung above the city that day. A bad day to sweat, a good day for the guys who had to roll Big Fatso into place on the Caddy and roll him off again.

"Waxie, I'd like chickuns tonight," Big Fatso said. "I haven't had a chickun I don' know when."

"You had chickuns Wednesday night," Waxie said. "You had 'um Thursday, too."

Big Fatso made a rumbling noise in his throat. A dark cloud drifted across his pumpkin face. Big Fatso didn't like anyone to tell him stuff that was different from the stuff inside his head. Even if the person was Maxie Lou Krimp, who was as cute as a bug at a trim two eighty-two, and looked real nice in her pink swimsuit and her bunny houseshoes.

"If I did have chickuns," Fatso said, "which I ain't sure I did, then I'll be having 'um some more. And I'd like some taters too. Tell Winky the beer he's been makin' is tasting like horse pee again. Tell him stop doing that. Tell him put somethin' in it don't taste like that. Tell Freak and Dinny I want 'um to off those clowns sold us all that bad pork. Tell 'um that sure ain't pork; tell 'um I know what it is and I won't put up with that. Tell C.R. I got twenty-two cases of Gut-

152

Rocker ammo I'm lettin' go cheap, seeing as how it kinda blows up you look at it twice. Tell him I got maybe fifty gross of camous hasn't even been used but one time and they ain't even shot up bad. And get them UN patches off of 'um first – the Congressionals and the 'Muricans, they don't neither one like that."

Maxie wrote it all down and left – or pretended that she did; where it was in her head. She'd never told Fatso she couldn't write a lick because Fatso had a weakness with an intellectual bent.

"Chickuns," Fatso muttered to himself. "Chickuns is what I want, and chickuns is what I'll by God get."

Chickuns were still on his mind while he finished off breakfast – two canned hams, three loaves of bread, two dozen eggs – fried – and pancakes he didn't stop to count. It was a breakfast only half a dozen people in all of Steel Harbor could afford. None of them ate as much as Fatso, but all of them – like Fatso himself – lived well outside the law.

He was sopping up the last of his import syrup when he heard the perimeter alarm. The alarm was Tommy Teeth clanging on a semi bumper hanging over the outside gate. It told Big Fatso that someone was coming in – not everyday commercial traffic, but someone of interest, someone he might want to see. Which, at the moment, wasn't anyone at all. He'd seen someone the day before and he was still tired out from that.

"Whoever it is," he yelled to Maxie, "tell Fixer to see 'um. I ain't in."

Maxie stuck her head in the door. "It's that's skinny-lookin' bitch, runs that joint in town."

153

Big Fatso raised an brow. "It's who?"

"You know who," Maxie said, giving him the nastiest look she could find, "don't go sayin' *who*."

"Barb Wire," Fatso said, careful to keep the tremor from his voice. "I bet that's who it is."

"Huh!" Maxie said. "I'll tell Fixer. He'll get her outta here quick."

"No, now don't do that, I better handle this," Fatso said quickly, "might be somethin' important. That woman's tricky, it comes to business shit."

"Monkey business is what it is," Maxie said. "Shoot, Fatso, what'd you do with a twit like that? She isn't hardly big as lunch."

Big Fatso decided not to answer that. Barb Wire would be gone again before the day was out and Maxie would still be there. Still, he hadn't always been seven-oh-three. He remembered slimmer days, and he remembered women nearly as break-your-heart gorgeous as the lovely Barb Wire.

Nearly as lovely. Not quite.

From a distance, Big Fatso's domain looked like a panorama of the Rockies. That is, if the Rockies were made of derelict cards, rusty scrap, assorted crap and gutted washing machines. Everything appeared tossed this way and that, with no apparent scheme of any sort. Anyone who tried to get into the place knew better than that. Big Fatso's wonderland of scrap was a junkyard fortress, a near impregnable maze of tunnels, moats, walls, halls, tripwires and traps. And if getting in was tough, getting out again was something else.

Barb Wire stopped her bike before the gate. The

154

gate itself was enough to intimidate all but the foolish and the truly brave of heart. It was thirty feet long and nine feet high, a rusty, ominous mass of rails from long-extinct trains, iron wheels and gears, radiators, generators, hubcaps and grilles, the whole of this stuck together by a lunatic welder on speed and decorated with nails, spikes, hooks and battle-wire.

The heavy gate rolled back on twenty-three bald-faced tires. Five of Fatso's Junkmen faced Barb. All were oversized, over-armed and mean as rabid bats.

"Hey-hey, Barb. Long time, huh?"

The man came toward her in a long and awkward lope. He was dressed in leather sewed together with scraps of wire. He was seven feet tall. His face, arms and chest were tattooed with lizards of every sort.

"You're looking good, Floyd," Barb said. "Is that a new cologne or you step in something back there?"

Floyd grinned, showing Jack-o'-lantern teeth. "Man, I sure like it when you talk like that. I get all – you know what."

"No, I don't know, Floyd, and don't you tell me either." She gunned her engine and waved a cloud of flies from her face. "We'll chat some other time, love, I've got to see Fatso now and you're standing in the road."

"Huh-uh. No way." Floyd shook his head and wrapped a dirty hand around the barrel of his gun. "I don't let nobody in here that's armed. You better give me that."

He nodded at the sawed-off shotgun strapped to Barb's bike.

Barb laughed. "You want me to do that? Did you get too much sun today, friend?"

155

"Hey, I'll give it back." Floyd looked pained. "It's the rules, Barb. You know that."

"Sure I do," Barb said. "Rules are rules, man." She reached for the shotgun, offered the butt to Floyd. Floyd stuck out his hand. Barb made a motion too quick to see – suddenly, the stock was in *her* hand, the twin barrels under Floyd's chin.

"D-damn, Barb!" Floyd swallowed hard. "Don't be doin' that!"

"I asked you real nice to stand aside. You didn't listen, Floyd."

Barb's finger tightened on the trigger. Floyd turned white. Barb squeezed and the weapon went *Click! Click!*

"Sh-shit!" Sweat ran down Floyd's face and stung his eyes.

Barb gave the shotgun a twirl and jammed it back in its holster.

"Forgot to load up. Must be your lucky day."

She revved the motor again and left Floyd standing. The other guards laughed, remarked on Floyd's failure as a man, gave several examples and generally ruined his day.

Barb guided her black machine through the narrow, twisted maze, past rusty walls so high they shut out the morning sun. She never saw a man; now and then she saw a woman or a child. The children were short and fat. The women wore ornaments of chrome and broken glass. One gave Barb a haughty look as she passed. A necklace of a hundred silver sparkplugs graced her neck.

From visits to Fatso's before, Barb was convinced

all the people looked alike. Skin the color of mud. Stringy black hair and tiny buckshot eyes.

Another generation in this dump and these people will be playing with their toes . . .

The maze opened out into a large, dirty-packed courtyard, relatively free of debris. She hadn't seen men on her way into the compound since all of them were here – a hundred, two hundred Floyds, in every shape and size. Some were clothed in hubcaps and jangled as they walked. Some were wrapped in copper wire. One sported dark heavy armor, carved out of Goodyear tires.

No one spoke. They stomped their feet and shook their fists. They hooted and they howled and they raped her with their eyes – made lewd remarks and gestured at their parts.

Barb totally ignored them, pretended that no one was there. A visit to the Junkmen was always a delight. As enriching as a day at the local dog pound.

She kept her eyes on the tallest structure around, a shabby tower built largely of the red and blue lights from ancient cop cars. Rumor had it that Fatso had tried to wire them all once, dreaming of fifty thousand Code Threes flashing in the night. There was no way to steal enough power, or no one in the Junkyard was smart enough to try.

Finally the rattle of a motor in terminal arrest came from the dark and narrow tunnel under the castle of the lights. A forklift wheezed into sight. Impaled on its prongs, like a great heap of dung in the jaws of an overworked bug, lay a customized sofa made of twelve backseats from Lincoln limousines. Sprawled, spilled, oozing from this throne was Big Fatso himself; rolled, wrapped, more or less encased in the threadbare curtain of the former peek-a-Boo adult movie palace on Steel Harbor's famous South Side.

Sitting beside Fatso was the lovely and full-figured Maxie Lou Krimp, adorned for the occasion in a shower curtain picturing colorful fish of tropic seas. Maxie gave Barb a hateful stare, and Barb returned a smile.

"Hey, Big Fatso," she said, "how's the king of crime, the scourge of the underworld? How's it hanging, man?"

"You wanna talk *bidness* with him, get on to it an' get the hell out," Maxie said. "But don' go infringin' on our personal private life!"

"Sorry, I get in the presence of greatness, I flat forget myself."

"Yeah, well don't," Maxie said.

It *was* an ill-chosen remark, Barb decided, and likely a sore point for Maxie Lou Krimp. If anything at all was "hanging" in regard to Big Fatso it would only be revealed after a long exhaustive search.

"It's real fine to see you," Big Fatso said. "And let me say you are looking –" he glanced quickly at Maxie – "uh, looking just fine."

"Shoot, you're too kind. I guess that's your nature and you can't help that."

Barb pulled a paper bag from her side saddle, crinkled up the top and tossed it at Fatso's throne.

"Just a small gesture. My way of showing respect, awe and gratitude."

Fatso caught the sack in his chubby fist. He peeked inside and a big grin creased his face.

"Donuts! Oh, Lordy, now where in shit city you

158

find somethin' like this? I ain't seen a real one, I don't know when."

"UN convoy. That red, purple, whatever kinda cross it is. Hit a Ripper mine. Scattered donuts and do-gooder ladies half a mile."

"Blessed be the fortunes of war," Fatso said, stuffing his face as fast as he could. When he was done he squeezed the sack and threw it over his shoulder, then dusted white powder off his hands.

"Might've been *poisoned* for all you know," Maxie grumbled.

"Might've been," Fatso said. "Lucky there wasn't none for you." He looked down at Barb. "Okay, you got me thinking kindly for a minute. Ain't about to last long. What you want here, Barb?"

"Business, Big Fatso. What else is going to bring me to this pesthole of yours? Meaning no offense."

Fatso threw back his head and laughed. When he laughed, everything around him laughed as well.

"Now that's the Barb Wire I know, by God." He punched Maxie in the ribs. "Is that the Barb Wire I know or what?"

"Yeah, it sure is," Maxie said. She made a face at Barb and squirreled a finger around a bad tooth.

"Somethin' told me, I don't know what," Fatso said, "that I'd be hearin' from you right soon."

"You're just uncanny, Fatso. It defies all reason. I don't know how you do it."

"Don't even try. The ways of intrigue and bidness is foreign to the female mind."

"You know us so well."

Fatso showed her a lazy smile. "Bar bidness okay? Everything going real fine?"

"You know how it is. *Comme ci, comme ca.*"

"Issat so?" Fatso raised a brow. "What with them pesky Con-gressionals breathin' down your neck, dangerous *fugitives* scratching at your door – what else we been hearing, Maxie?"

"Search warrants. Ever'thing getting busted up."

"Right, friggin' *search* warrants. I plain forgot." Fatso shook his head. "With all that going on, I'd say you ain't real commy-sea, or that other thing, neither."

"Trouble comes, trouble passes."

"Sometimes it just comes."

"There's that." Barb shrugged. "I'm impressed you're so well informed, Fatso, but I didn't come to hear what's going on with me. I've got a proposition. You want to hear it or not?"

"He don't need no propositions from skinnys," Maxie said. "He's doin' fine the way he is."

Fatso ignored her. He raised one finger and the forklift slipped him down close to Barb. The sun vanished behind his back. Barb felt slightly sick. It was like being swallowed by the biggest grub worm in the world.

"You correct me if I'm off base now," Fatso said. "It's just a wild guess, isn't nothin' more'n that. This *proposition* doesn't have anything to do with some kinda *lenses*, now does it?"

"Lenses? I wouldn't know about any lenses." Barb tried to look confused, but Fatso knew better than that.

"Don't go wastin' any time on theatricals with me. I don't figure you came all the way into the heart of my evil empire to bring me some friggin' donuts."

"Like I say, I am so in awe of your powers." Barb batted her eyes. "The truth is, I'm in a sort of position, at the moment, to broker the sale of those lenses you mentioned."

Fatso beamed. "That's exactly what I heard. An' I wouldn't have believed it if it hadn't come from a what-you-call-it – an un-peckable source."

Fatso raised one hand as if he were waving off flies. On the ground, a few feet from Barb, a short, fiery-whiskered Junkman opened a rusty refrigerator door. He tilted it slightly, and a very stiff Rhino Schmitz tumbled out.

"I guess you two have met," Fatso said.

"He looks so lifelike," Barb said, "except for being dead."

Fatso laughed again and nearly shook the forklift off its wheels.

"All *right*," he said, clapping his meaty hands. "Oh, Lord, I love bidness, let's make a deal!"

Twenty-three

The dark didn't bother him anymore. In the beginning, it had bothered him a lot. Hell, it had scared him half to death, driven him out of his ever-loving skull. If it hadn't been for guys in the outfit, and couple of good docs, and Barb, of course, Charlie would have blown his brains out. He even gave it a couple of good tries, but a blind man is at a disadvantage when it comes to things like that. You can't find a weapon or anything to hang yourself with, the only real danger you're in is falling on your ass.

Before he got good enough to do any damage to himself, he discovered the benefit of drugs and alcohol. He mixed the two for a while, threw up a lot. Found the booze worked fine by itself, and tossed the drugs aside. By working overtime, it didn't take long before he reached the status of certified drunk.

It suited him fine. Not everything was clear all the time, sometimes he wasn't too sure where he was – or even who – but then, that was the whole idea. The booze dulled the present – and most of all, the past – and Charlie didn't care about the future anymore. With any luck at all, he figured when it got there he'd be gone.

Drink dulled his senses. And the dark made them keen. In time, Charlie found he could hear, smell, feel – sense things he had never even thought about before. He had always been great with this hands; he had the knack, he knew where things belonged. He could take things apart and put them back together again.

Now, though, he no longer merely worked with a piece of machinery, an electronic device. Now he felt as if he were a *part* of that device – that his mind, his hands, and a sense he couldn't define, that all these things were one. When he fixed Barb's bikes he became both the tools and the parts, the throb of the engine, the heart and the soul of the metal beast itself. And sometimes he was sure that he left some part of himself in every machine he touched, that he gave every cable and gear, every link of chain and strip of chrome, a strength that it hadn't had before, and that the machine, in turn, gave something back to him.

And then again, he told himself, he was a drunk, and a lot of this mysterious crap was in his head, and had no link to reality at all . . .

He had been in the maze before. You didn't need eyes in there, you needed to smell, you needed to feel and hear. You needed to feel the flow of air, hear the scuttering of the rats, hear the echo of your touch along the walls.

Even before he turned the corner, felt the narrow passage give way to open space, he knew something was wrong. Knew, with a chill that warned every nerve in his body, every cell, that nothing was right anymore, that nothing was the way it ought to be.

"Spike?"

He spoke the name softly, spoke it in fear, said the name and knew, knew as sure as death itself, she couldn't answer, knew that she was there, and knew where.

He went to his knees, let the faint, sweet and terrible scent guide him across the stone floor. His hands touched what they were seeking, drew back, hesitated, touched again. A leather boot, a bare leg, all the flesh bare above that. He was careful to avoid the private places, careful to show respect. His hands shook as he felt the familiar face, the skin still warm, felt the angular nose, felt the ring there. He touched her forehead, felt the slight wetness, the indentation where the bullet had kissed her between the eyes.

God, Spike, I'm sorry. I'm dreadfully sorry for us all . . .

"I want you to share with me, Charlie," said the voice across the room. "There're things I gotta know, and I'd be real grateful if you'd tell 'em to me now . . ."

Twenty-four

"Two million," Barb said, "that's it. I'm not having a sale today, Fatso. I've got other places I can go."

"One-five or you can ride out of here. I didn't just fall off the wagon, my dear."

"One million. Final. Period. No phony-baloney money. Canadian bucks."

Big Fatso grinned. "Deal."

"Shit," Maxie said, "she would've took less than that."

"Shut up," Fatso said, "I'm doin' bidness here." He shook his head at Barb. "It's goin' to take a while to get my hands on that much Canadian money. You'll have to give me a day, maybe two."

"Huh-unh. No way." Barb folded her arms. "There's a plane I got to catch. It leaves from the old airport on the other side of the unoccupied zone."

Fatso made a face. "I don't like the unoccupied zone. Bad part of town."

Barb laughed. "Fatso, *you're* a bad part of town. Here's what I want. *Safe* passage for me and Charlie. That's a full escort on the way to the airport. I'm talking the best of these bozos you've got, first-rate armor, the works. And you handle the tolls."

Fatso rolled his eyes and gave a great sigh. It was a gesture that set waves of fat in motion, a tremor that shook the makeshift sofa, the forklift truck, and nearly knocked Maxie off her perch.

"Like I said, I don't care for this *at* all. Ever'thing's real unpredictable, you start messin' around in the zone. No telling what you'll find, or what'll find you. That toll collector's a son of a bitch, too. And if the Resistance folks find out what I'm doin' . . ."

Barb slammed her fists against her sides. "Damn you, Fatso, don't think I don't know what you're doing 'cause I do. And it isn't going to work, okay?"

Fatso looked hurt. "What? What am I doing, I'm not doin' a thing."

"You're trying to screw me outta money, that's what."

"I'm not doing any such thing. I'm thinking *adjustment*, is all."

"Adjustment."

"Something of this nature, trouble could arise and we'd all be eating armor-piercin' pie. I'm going to have to use an extra vehicle or two. I'm sure going to have to put on some more men . . ." Fatso closed one eye in thought. "I'm seeing, this is the figure I'm seeing, safe passage guaranteed, and *half* a million Canadian bucks."

"Eight-fifty."

"Six."

"Seven-fifty," Barb said. "Up front."

"Done. And let me say I am right proud to get strung up by a bidness person as sly and astute as yourself." Fatso extended a chubby hand. "Let's have those lenses. Lord, you'll put me in the poorhouse, Barb, but I guess I deserve what I get, letting you pin me to the ground."

Barb slapped her forehead. "What do I look like – I just got hatched, I'm going to give 'em to you *here*? I'll meet you at the first toll, an hour before sundown. Cash for the merchandise, right there."

She jabbed a finger in his direction. "If you are five minutes late I am *out* of there, I am off to another buyer."

"Now that hurts." Big Fatso laid a hand on his heart. "You've got no cause to talk to me like that."

"Yeah, you got no cause to talk to him like that," Maxie Lou said. "You ought to be 'shamed of yourself."

A low murmur swept the crowd at Barb's back. It sounded like a herd of angry cows. Barb didn't bother to turn around.

"That outfit, Maxie, that's you. You ought to wear it all the time."

Maxie looked puzzled. "Why, I do."

"Right," Barb said. She slammed her boot down hard on the starter. The big hog came to life with a roar. The wheels whined, Barb shot Fatso a casual salute and left a plume of dust in her wake.

"I swear," Maxie said, "I don't know what's happening. People ain't nice like they used to be, hon."

"It's the times," Fatso told her. He thought about Barb, thought about the way she looked racing down the road, thought about the way all her parts stayed firm and nice, nothing shaking out of place at all.

"It's the times, Maxie Lou, is what it is. Hasn't anybody got no friggin' values anymore . . ."

The country was *not* in any danger, we were *not* falling apart. That is not just my opinion, I can back it up with facts. The economy was going through a slight period of adjustment, a very normal fluctuation that would certainly have straightened itself out. It always has – that's the nature of economics. You're up and then you're down, and then you're up again.

There were, at the time the Congressional traitors forcibly took control of the government, a few people out of jobs. There are *always* people out of jobs. Sometimes more, and sometimes less. *Everyone* can't have a job, when did everyone have a job, tell me that? And there were, at the time, some people who were rich, some people who were poor. Maybe that's not fair, but was it ever any other way – anywhere, any time? Our Founding Fathers weren't Communists – they created a nation where everyone had the opportunity to be better than somebody else. It would be just fine if every American could be a millionaire, but it just doesn't work that way.

We had a certain amount of inequality along racial and ethnic lines. Again, that's not right, and I would like to note that my administration was doing everything in its power to erase those differences and bring all our people together.

We had a national debt – no one's denying that. And it wasn't getting any smaller, that's a fact. We had a crime problem, a drug problem, a population problem, a traffic problem. We had all kinds of problems. We also had all of our cities intact, instead of a lot of holes in the ground. We didn't have a nation divided, we didn't have millions of people dead. We didn't have tyranny throughout the land. We didn't have famine and disease. We didn't have Congressional storm troopers tramping through our streets.

All right, so the country wasn't perfect. So take a good look at it now. And, while I don't mean to offend, my fellow citizens, I'd like you to remember one thing: *You* voted those sons of bitches into office in the first place, not me . . .

[Excerpt from an illegal broadcast by the former President of the United States of America.]

– Johnny Gray Wolf, PhD, *Fall From Glory* (2032),
University of the New Sioux Nation Press.

Twenty-five

"*Charlie Kopetski, you are charged with concealing information regarding the whereabouts of a certain pair of contact lenses. Said lenses are vital to the national security of the Congressional Republic. We would most strongly urge you to cooperate to the utmost in this matter.*

"*You are being held for questioning by duly authorized officials of the Congressional Republic. You have been formally requested to answer certain questions put to you by said officials. Your failure to do so has caused delays in the pursuit of justice, and, regrettably, a certain amount of physical and mental discomfort to yourself. Let it be noted for the record that you endure this discomfort of your own accord, and that the Congressional Republic takes no responsibility for any temporary and/or permanent damage brought about through your refusal to perform your duty as a citizen. Once again, I must urge you to urgeyoutourgeyoutourge   urgeyouto*
       urrrrrrrrggggttttttooo . . .
         urrrrrrrgg . . .
             urrrrrrrrrrrrrrrrrrrrrrrrrrrr . . ."

The voice had been talking to him forever. The voice didn't speak to him in words. The voice said "*urrrrrrrrrrrrrrrr . . . urrrrrr . . . urrrrrrrr . . .*"

It sounded like a broken fan, like the lazy drone of insects on a hot afternoon.

They hurt him real bad . . .

When they did, he screamed and cried out and begged them to let him go. God, it hurt bad. It hurt even worse than it did when the mine went off and took his eyes. That didn't hurt much at all, at the time. Not when it happened. But it hurt like hell after that. He never told Barb but it still hurt bad sometimes.

Barb?

Sis, are you there? I sure need you now . . .

Well, shit, of course she wasn't there. Lord God, he hoped she wasn't there! He couldn't stand it, couldn't take it for a minute if they hurt his sister like this. He'd tell them anything, then. Tell them about the goddamn lenses, tell them about Axel and Cora D. – tell them anything they wanted if they wouldn't do anything to Barb . . .

They turned on the pain again. He felt his muscles tense, felt a bone snap somewhere as his body twitched out of control, slamming him back against the chair. He howled like a dog until his throat went raw, then they cut the pain off and he flowed back down into the blessed dark again . . .

"What the hell's wrong with the screen, mister? All I'm seeing is static, it's not picking up a damn thing!"

"He's blind, Colonel. He doesn't process visual data. People who are born blind never have it, of course. And many people who lose their sight eventually forget what it was like to see. Without continued stimulation, the memory is –"

"I didn't ask for a Mr. Science lecture, Landdale. Just *do* something. I don't give a shit if he can *see* the lenses or not. I want to know where they are!"

"Sir, I don't recommend it. If we keep it up we're going to lose him. The EKG shows some bad fluctuations now . . ."

Pryzer glared. "Did you hear me, am I gettin' through to you, mister?"

"Yes, sir. I –"

"Then get on it, son. *Now*!"

Pryzer leaned down close to Charlie. Charlie's face was gray as ash. His sweat smelled sour; it smelled like it always did on a man in his condition, it smelled like fear. He'd dirtied himself early on. Nearly everyone did. They'd plucked the silver wires off his chest and hosed him off twice. The smell always came back. You could burn out their skulls but you couldn't stop the smell.

"Charlie . . . Charlie, now I know you are in there somewhere, you are hidin' from me, and I don't like you doing that. You *talk* to me, you hear?"

Pryzer hesitated. He looked at Charlie, then glanced at the screen. Nothing. The crackle of static, nothing on the monitor at all. Something, a feeling, an itch, made him look at the operator. The operator quickly looked away.

Now why'd he do that? A man doesn't look at me, there's something he doesn't want me to see . . .

Pryzer jerked up and faced the man, saw the color leave his face. He shoved the man roughly aside, squinted at the power dial, saw at once what the man had done.

"Well, you sorry son of a bitch!" The colonel

grabbed him by the collar, lifted him off his feet and tossed him back across the room. The man yelled, hit a chair and fell on his back.

"Don't want to *hurt* anyone, now do we? Don't want to make the prisoner *uncomfortable* or anything. Shit!"

Pryzer began inching the power dial up the scale. Charlie Kopetski started dancing in his chair. The chair hopped across the floor. Charlie's body jerked. Muscle tore and bone snapped. His skin began to scorch and turn black where the silver wires met his chest.

"Where are those lenses, son? Tell me where!"

Blood poured from Charlie's mouth. Blood came out of his nose and ears.

"WHERE ARE THE LENSES, YOU BASTARD? I AM TALKING TO YOU!"

Charlie Kopetski didn't answer.

Charlie didn't know he was dancing in his chair, didn't know his bones were breaking, didn't know his flesh was on fire. All Charlie knew was he'd found the greatest bar in the world, a bar with the very coolest sounds, the very tallest women, the oldest whiskey anywhere, and he didn't need those friggin' black glasses anymore, he could see just fine, he could see a lot better than he'd ever seen before . . .

Twenty-six

"I guess you've thought about this," Curly said. "I guess you know what you're doing."

"I've thought about it," Barb said. "I gave it a good three minutes. And no, I *don't* know what I'm doing. What the hell has that got to do with anything?"

Curly leaned on his broom and gave Barb a dismal sigh.

"Nothing, I don't guess. I'd just like to see somethin' happen once in my life that made sense. You running off like this, that sure isn't it."

Barb came up against him, hugged him and planted a kiss on his mouth. Curly blinked and looked stunned. Part of a dream had come true, probably as close as he was ever going to get. The rest he'd have to do in his head, but he was used to that.

Barb turned and started opening drawers, yanking things out, tossing some on the bed, tossing most on the floor – boots, ammo, frothy underwear. She stared at a motorcycle part. Looked at it, turned it one way then the next. Now where the hell was that supposed to go?

Muttering to herself, she slammed the drawers shut and plopped herself in a chair.

"You're right, Curly, I'm flat nuts. I don't know why I'm going through that stuff since I'm not packing *anything*. I need something, I'll get it new. My

God, if they haven't got it in Paris I probably don't want it. We –" Barb stopped, frowned at Curly and shook her head. "Now I want you to flat stop that, you hear? Just stop it right now."

"Stop what? I'm not doing anything."

"Stop lookin' like a dog that just got hit by a truck. Hell's fire, Curly . . ."

She stood and went to him again, took both his hands in hers.

"You're losing me, you're gaining a bar," she said gently. "That's a real good deal, you know?"

"No, it's not, either." He pulled away and stared at the floor. "I'm a waiter, for Christ's sake. I know how to – how to wait, and that's it."

"You'll catch on fast. The difference between waiting and owning is you get to keep the money the help doesn't steal, and you fire 'em when they do."

"That isn't it and you know it." Curly scratched his stubbly chin. "I know better than that."

"Well, of course you do. That's why you're going to be fine." She glanced at her watch. "Come on, give me a hand with this thing. I've got to get out of here."

Curly set his broom aside and joined her across the room. Barb took one end of her heavy four-poster bed and Curly took the other. Camille, who was sprawled on a satin pillow, opened one eye, gave Barb an irritated look and hopped to the floor.

With the bed shoved aside, Barb got down on her knees and moved a loose floorboard an inch to the left, then half an inch to the right. The paneling on the wall above slid aside to reveal a metal roll-up door. A light went on and cool air rushed into the room.

A van stood on the concrete floor. It was squat,

black, totally nondescript. The fenders were artfully dented, the paint was carefully chipped. It weighed three times more than it should, had a modified aircraft engine, and its armor would stop nearly anything smaller than a Blisterbutt shell. Charlie had built it from the ground up. Barb had told him it was a pure waste of time, that she was damned if they'd ever leave the Hammerhead, ever need to run. Charlie just told her she was probably right, but you never could tell.

You're right and I was wrong, little brother . . . You never can tell . . .

Barb opened the driver's door and climbed in. The van smelled new. It wasn't, but Charlie had a thing about that, and sprayed it "new" every day.

"I don't like this," Curly said. "I'm going to – damn it, I'm going to miss you guys."

"I'm going to miss you too. Don't forget to lock up, not that it does any good. And be nice to Camille or I'll come *back*, you hear?"

"Promise?"

Barb grinned and looked at her watch again. "Damn it, Charlie, we got to get out of here." She blew a strand of hair from her face. "Probably trying to find all his *tools*. Like they're really looking for blind mechanics in France . . ."

"Oh, he said he had to say goodbye. I thought I told you that."

"What? No, you didn't tell me that, Curly. You're going to run the Hammerhead, you got to start remembering things."

"Said he was going to – you know, say goodbye to a friend."

"And what friend would that be?"

"I forget." Curly bit his lip. "Spike? Charlie know somebody named Spike?"

War brings the expected, and the unexpected as well. Death, famine, disease and horror are the natural offspring of armed conflict. The unexpected often takes strange and unusual form.

In the aftermath of the Second American Civil War, the people of this country were no longer obsessed with household pets. During the worst of the famine years, animals formerly called "Fluffy" and "Spot" were frequently called "lunch". While hungry people had no regrets for such actions at the time, the long-term psychological damage was intense.

After the war, when those dogs and cats that had survived began to return to populated areas, there were few who could face them without recalling the terrible days of puppy traps and kitty snares, of moments of joy and delight when Daddy checked the lines and said, "I got the little bastard this time!"

Many incidents of PWPD (Post-War Pet Depression) resulted in serious mental and physical disorders. There were, as well, a number of suicides directly related to this condition.

Many former pets, of course, did not return from the wilds at all, but remained in dangerous packs, preying upon each other and what few animals remained – squirrel, rabbit, and the wary herds of savage cows. Some packs were said to take a special

interest in seeking out their former masters,
but a great many of these reports were
exaggerated or totally untrue.

– Johnny Gray Wolf, PhD, *Fall From Glory* (2032),
University of the New Sioux Nation Press.

Twenty-seven

Axel listened.

There was no lack of things to listen to; there were sounds all around, sounds everywhere. He didn't know which was worse – too much or nothing at all. Nothing at all was pretty bad. In combat, silence was by far the most frightening sound of all. You knew there was something out there. You didn't dare believe you were alone, because then maybe *you'd* make a noise and they'd know for certain exactly where you were. And when you didn't hear something for a very long time, you had to hear something, so you made something up. After two or three nerve-screaming nights you were so friggin' rattled you couldn't tell the difference between the sounds outside and the ones inside your head.

That's when they got you. That's when some mother crawled in your hole and the next thing you knew you were flat-ass dead . . .

"Snakers, I think," he whispered to Corrina. "Two of 'em, over by that caved-in store. They must be hungry, spookin' around in the light."

Corrina trembled against him. "Will they bother us, you think – will they come over here?"

"No, they won't. Because they don't know we're here."

He didn't tell her that the Snakers were so good

that if they did know he and Corrina were there they'd have a fair chance of getting in so close he'd never have a chance to open fire – that even in broad daylight, in the afternoon sun, they were deadlier than most men with all their arms and legs. Corrina didn't need to hear that. She had enough to be frightened of now.

Axel paused, listened to a car in the distance, the flat crack of automatic fire. The sounds were far off and died away.

"If anyone's watching, I think they'd make a move by now," he told Corrina. "We've got to chance it anyhow, we've got to let them know."

Corrina took a deep breath. "Of course. Let's go."

He ran low and fast, keeping the heavy K-50 clutched at his waist, the snout sweeping the rubble-filled street ahead. Corrina followed on his heels, holding the .45 at her side. It was an out-of-date weapon, but it had served her well so far. In a spare moment Axel had taken it from her and ground off the shine.

He ducked quickly into the shadow of the door-way. The door to the Resistance hidey-hole was unlocked, as usual, and that told him nothing at all.

If the goons have found the place they'll be in there waiting for anyone dumb enough to show up. If they're here they've got us in their goddamn sights right now . . .

"We get inside, I'm using a light," he told her. "Probably a bad idea, but I'm not groping through that maze again. Just in case."

Corrina gave him a sober look. "Axel, I am not mentally deficient. If the Congressionals have found the place we'll get about ten bloody feet. I know that."

"Yeah. I know you do."

"Good. Then do whatever you have to do."

"Corrina, I didn't mean any –"

"I know you didn't. You're a protector. That's what you do, Axel. You protect. Twenty-four hours a day. And you do it very well."

"That remains to be seen," he said. "Tell me that when we –"

Axel stopped, cursed and pushed Corrina inside. The van had rolled past the corner, its engine turned off, suddenly catching them there yakking, too close to run.

Dropping to his knee, he brought the K-50 to his shoulder, took a deep breath . . .

"I am getting too old for this shit, Axel. Will you please put that down?"

Axel blinked. "Barb? My God, is that you?"

Barb brought the van to a halt, opened the door and slid out.

"If it's not, you're sorta *dead*, don't you think?"

She looked past him to the door, saw Corrina there, looked at Axel again, this time caught the look in his eyes.

"What the hell are you two doing here? What is it, Axel?" She pushed him roughly aside, stomped through the door. "Goddamn it, goddamn everyone!"

"We heard the Congressionals had maybe scoped the place out," he called after her, "that's why we're here. We don't know that, Barb."

Barb didn't answer. She ran through the maze, her

flash sweeping ahead, her free hand white on the grip of her gun. He didn't need to tell her, she'd known the instant she saw his face, she'd seen that look a thousand times before, the haunted stance, the look of men going in somewhere they might not come out of again . . .

Oh God, don't be in there, Charlie, don't be in there, love . . . don't – don't – don't!

She didn't see him, she saw the others first. Some of them were lined up face down, lined up neatly in a row. Their hands were tired behind their backs; they'd been shot execution style.

That wasn't as bas as the ones still sitting up. Twelve of them, seated in the courtroom's ruined jury box. All of them looking straight ahead. All of them with a neat, single hole between the eyes.

Pryzer, you bastard, you sick son of a bitch. If I stay alive then you're dead . . .

She found Spike and saw what had happened there. Charlie wasn't far away. He was on his side and they'd left him strapped to the chair. Barb went down on her knees, drew her knife, cut his bonds away and took him in her arms. She held him, hugged him to her breast, talked to him, let the hot tears scald her cheeks, let them fall on Charlie's ruined eyes.

She took off her jacket and used it to clean his face, to wipe the dirt away. His hair was caked with blood, and she smoothed it out gently, brushing it off his face.

You don't have to do it anymore, little brother, you don't have to fight . . . we get to Paris, I'll make it up to you, Charlie, I swear to God I will . . .

Axel touched Corrina's shoulder and stopped. Corrina drew in a sharp breath and whispered to herself, words Axel couldn't hear.

Axel came to Barb's side. A shaft of sunlight pierced the shattered roof, brightened Barb's yellow hair, found the concrete floor and Charlie's bloodless face.

"I'm sorry," Axel said. "Damn it, Barb, if I could've been here sooner . . ."

She looked past him somewhere, a thousand miles away. The tears dried on her cheeks. Her face, her eyes, showed no emotion at all.

"He's dead. He doesn't care what you think or I think anymore. He doesn't care."

"Miss Wire . . ." Corrina stepped up beside Axel. "I know you don't – everybody doesn't feel the same way about this fight, and I don't blame anyone for that. You, and me, Axel, we've all got to go our own way. But if you don't mind me intruding, I'm going to say your brother had his feelings too, real strong feelings, and I'm guessing that dying for them would be all right with him. I hope you don't mind me speaking out. I don't have any right . . ."

Barb didn't answer. She looked at Corrina a long moment, then gazed across the room and past it.

"I'm not going to be polite," Axel said, "I'm going to go ahead and ask. I don't suppose you can have any worse feelings about me than you do now –"

Barb's head came up fast, her eyes full of fire.

"That's what's wrong with you, Axel Hood, you think you know everything there is. You damn sure thought you knew everything about *me*. Hell, mister, you didn't even get a good start. You were so *full* of

184

it, thinkin' you had Barbara Kopetski down flat, you missed about half the good parts."

She wiped Charlie's face once more, kissed him gently on the cheek and laid her jacket across his face. She stood, then, facing Axel and Corrina.

"That plane of yours. We got – what? My watch got broken somewhere."

"Ninety minutes," Axel said. "I don't know how we'll get there on time, get through the Zone –"

Barb gave him a weary laugh. "That's what I was saying, Axel. You don't know everything. You're goddamn lucky I do . . ."

Twenty-eight

The black van rolled through the ruined streets, past the crumbling buildings, the tin and paper shacks, past the craters and the burned-out cars. The sun was a boil on the sickly evening sky.

Axel got the picture right away. You didn't have to be too bright to see Barb's van was more than it seemed to be. As he slid into the wide, cushioned seat between Corrina and Barb, he took in the armor-glass, the heavy safety bars. He could sense the van's weight, knew the shocks were strong enough to take a fall that would kill everyone inside.

The dash looked like a panel of a Buzz-Saw fighter plane. He wondered if the damn thing could fly. Barb likely thought it would, and he hoped to God she wouldn't try.

Behind the seat, arranged in snug, padded rows along the walls were enough arms to start a small war: Laser-Chaser Tens, Go-Go Bombs the size of silver tennis balls, Raker automatics, Chinese Kopi-Kat Glocks, and a double case of Screamo grenades.

"Nice car," Axel said.

"Thought you might like it," Barb said. "Only thing is, mileage is awful bad."

"Does the word *overkill* ring a bell with you?"

"You ever try to get out of Steel Harbor?"

"I don't suppose I ever did."

"Then shut up and let me drive."

Axel slumped down in his seat and risked a look at Corrina. Corrina was biting her lips white. Barb slammed the van into a gear Alex hadn't ever thought about before. The van screamed around a corner at a speed that would have rolled a Viper tank. It hugged the road hard and not a wheel left the ground.

"How far have we got to go?" Axel frowned at his watch. "To the plane, I mean."

"Not far. Far's not the problem."

"So what is?"

"The toll. The toll is the problem."

Axel gave her a curious look. "The toll? We've got a problem with the toll?"

"Axel, leave me the hell alone. Let me drive, okay?"

"No. Not okay." He turned in the seat to face her. "I like to know where I'm going before I get there. An old habit I learned in the field. I need a couple of seconds' notice if I'm supposed to maybe duck, shoot someone, shit like that."

"You want a lot," Barb said.

"Something else I want. I want to know where the lenses are. I appreciate what you're doing, but I'd like to get that straightened out right now."

"They're safe."

"I didn't ask you that. Corrina can't get on the plane without the lenses. What are you waiting for? Let's have 'em now, Barb."

"Axel . . ."

Corrina gripped his arm. "You heard her. Let her alone, let her drive."

"Damn it, we haven't got time to play games!"

187

"Listen to the lady," Barb said. "She's giving you good advice."

Axel clenched his fists at his sides. He was fully prepared to jump in the fight again. That's the way it had always been between them, no reason it should start to change now.

Corrina looked at him and shook her head. Axel scooted down in his seat and muttered to himself. That part hadn't changed, either. Barb could always hold out longer, always wear him out.

Barb raced the van through the near empty streets. Another night was coming on, and anyone who had a good strong, solid door was shutting it up tight.

As the day faded behind bilious clouds, the outskirts of Steel Harbor gave way to a flat nearly featureless landscape of rubble, dead vegetation and the twisted stumps of trees. For a mile or more, nothing stood higher than a foot above the ground. It looked like a plain of desolation, a place where a fierce and deadly battle had taken place.

The desolation here, though, was deliberate and calculated. Every tree, every building, had been razed to the ground to make it impossible for any creature larger than a rat to get in and out of Steel Harbor without being seen. And, to make the point perfectly clear, halfway across these dead and arid flats, a sign read:

**YOU ARE NOW LEAVING
THE U.N.-PROTECTED AREA.
PROCEED AT YOUR OWN RISK.**

188

Beyond that was a brief stretch of nothing called the Unoccupied Zone. Past that was the war. Currently, all the territory surrounding Steel Harbor was in the hands of the Congressionals. A battle might start at any moment, however, and the situation would change for a day or a week, until one general or another decided to toss more lives into the game.

Living in Steel Harbor, someone said, was like living in a tent soaked in gasoline in the middle of an ammo dump, surrounded by ten million madmen tossing matches across the fence.

Corrina looked at the sign as they passed. The fact that the words "UN" and "PROTECTED" had been nearly blown away by a shotgun blast did little to settle her nerves.

It had all seemed so reasonable before. Get to Steel Harbor, make contact with the Resistance there, get the lenses and get out. It was risky, of course – but what hadn't been risky since she'd been on the run? At least this was a chance worth taking, to get to Canada and expose the Congressionals' plan, let the whole world know about Red Ribbon.

Now, so close to that day, the moment when freedom was in her grasp, Corrina Devonshire felt that she was hurtling back into the storm with every mile – that she was not sitting safely in an armored van, she was trapped in a portable tomb. That the last thing she'd see before they fried her in there was Barb Wire laughing in her face, telling her what a damn fool she'd been . . .

It had all happened so quickly, and Corrina had never felt more joyous, more full of life. You could sense the excitement in the air, feel the press of great events. And she was there when it happened, in the nation's capital itself, right there as the great drama of revolution unfolded day by day, hour by hour.

She abhorred the bloody riots, of course, the street battles that raged around DC between the New Congressional Army and the dissident American forces. That was a part of revolution, though, Carl told her – not a pleasant part, for certain, but it was something that had to be. It wouldn't last long, and then they could all get on with creating a new society, the kind of country America was meant to be when the founders of our nation fought another war to set us free.

Carl was right, she knew. It all happened the way he said it would – the House and the Senate confronting the President with demands for change, the challenges, the bitter confrontations. And finally, inevitably, the Declaration of Congress, the document that set forth in bold and certain terms the demand for total government reorganization, changes that would set the United States of America on a course that would see its citizens once more in control of their destinies.

The President had balked at what he called "outrageous change that would lead the nation not into better times, but would bury our basic freedoms forever."

The President's protests went largely unnoticed. Congress had done its job well, and the people were ready for change – that's what they'd been promised and they were ready for it now – not later, not in due course, right *now*.

"Even if we have to revert to force, it's got to happen," Carl said. "The voting booth didn't work, we've by God got to try something else!"

Corrina believed it because Carl said it was so. Carl believed so strongly in the Congressional cause you couldn't be near him without believing too. That was one of the things she loved about him – there was nothing halfway about Carl, not in his convictions, not in the way he loved her. His passions were overpowering in every aspect of his life.

She would never forget the way he had looked in his dress blacks, a new lieutenant in the Congressional Marines. They had champagne that night, a rare and expensive treat now that very few products from overseas were allowed under the Congressional trade bans. That was something that had to be, though, Carl said. Everyone had to make sacrifices to bring the nation back to a first-rate power. Foreign countries had been bleeding us dry too long, and that was coming to an end, along with outside ownership of American business and industry. Everything wouldn't happen at once, Carl said. But it *would* happen, he was certain of that.

There were shortages to get used to, and a lot of the new rules and regulations you had to live under seemed overly harsh sometimes, but there was a purpose in that, she knew. Though there were times – and she never discussed this with Carl – when it seemed that life under Congressional rule was *too* hard, more restrictive than it really had to be. That a lot of the new "Articles of Freedom" didn't seem much like freedom at all.

After Carl's unit was called up to quell the

Arkansas Uprising, Corrina sometimes found it hard to accept the hardships of daily life. Carl wasn't there to explain how important it was to give up things personally for the greater good of the country, that the privileges we might be giving up now would return to them tenfold when the war was over and done.

There was one thing in particular that bothered her a great deal. The "minor, isolated outbreaks" they'd been told to expect in the beginning had turned out to be anything but minor – or isolated, either. One conflict had led to another, until the country was engaged in a bloody, full-scale civil war. The armed forces of the United States had not caved in or come over to the Congressionals as expected. Instead they had fought, and fought fiercely. Millions of men were dead on either side, and a lot of American cities lay in ruin.

It wouldn't last much longer, though, they said on TV. The US Forces and the Resistance units would have to throw in the towel soon.

Only they didn't. They kept on fighting. And, all across the nation, men kept on dying.

With Carl gone, Corrina tried to lose herself in her work. Medical research was important, and Corrina was highly respected in her field. There were privileges and extra rations for such people, and Corrina, like most everyone else, found them hard to turn down. And if she happened to see Congressional troopers stop citizens on the street and question them in a somewhat violent manner, she told herself those persons might well be traitors or war profiteers who deserved whatever they got. It didn't help, though, that the troopers who patrolled the streets wore the same Congressional armbands and the same black uniforms that Carl wore.

She couldn't imagine Carl treating people like that, even if it might be the right thing to do.

Carl's letters quit coming. She knew that he'd write if he could. If he didn't, she knew something was terribly wrong.

Something was. They sent Carl home in a box. At least, they told her it was Carl. Anyone who'd heard what happened at Stone Mountain knew that no one but God himself would ever identify the hundred thousand Americans and Congressionals who died there. Any time it gets hotter than the sun about a mile and a half away, there isn't much need for body bags . . .

After that, Corrina quit feeling anymore. On the outside, she was still Corrina. She did her job and did it well, worked on the projects they gave her, worked until she dropped and they made her go home. Inside, though, she was hollow – hollow and dead. Inside, there was very little left.

She didn't think about Carl. She didn't think about anything at all. Everyone talked about the war, but she closed her mind to that. She heard the long silence, the sound that is no sound at all. What she heard was the sound of the dead. They were marching, marching in a long, dark line, a line that seemed to stretch out forever, a line with no beginning, a line with no end . . .

It was a cold night in March, the wind burning her flesh, bringing tears to her eyes. She ducked her head inside her coat and hurried up the steps of the research building. No one challenged her, the guard merely nodded and let her by and hurried back out of the cold. Dr. Corrina Devonshire had a Priority Double A: she could come and go as she liked and often did.

She had decided to kill herself at work. Not because she was overly fond of her home. There was nothing there she cared about, now that Carl was gone. She decided to kill herself at the office because they would find her immediately there. Someone would show up at her house in a few days, but she didn't like to think about that. She was a doctor, after all, and she knew what happened to a body after a very short while.

She wasn't supposed to have the .45. No one was supposed to have arms anymore, you were supposed to turn them in. The weapon had been her father's, though, and his father's before that. Even if you were ready to lose yourself it was hard to let everything go.

She had the clip in the gun and a shell jacked in the chamber. She was sitting at her desk. She didn't like to leave things undone and she was going through her computer once more, looking for anything she didn't want anyone to see. She seldom made personal notes of any kind, but sometimes she'd tap something in she thought she should remember, something she still had to do about Carl. Not that there was much. He only had a sister, and she'd taken care of what little there was to fill out. If they'd ever gotten married, then there'd be all kind of things to do, but they'd never gotten around to that. What for? They loved each other, they were together every minute they could spare. They had the rest of their lives, there was plenty of time for rituals and ceremonies, why waste time on that?

Corrina stopped, then, the after-image of something catching her eye. Something out of place, something that didn't belong at all.

She backed up, found it again. It was a formula, or a part of one, anyway – just the beginning, the rest of it gone. It was something she'd never seen before, or anything like it. It wasn't a project she was working on, and she was dead certain no one else in the department was involved in *anything* like this. My God, if anyone dared to follow those lines, to actually bring something like that into being!

Corrina's blood ran cold. She knew, at once, that was exactly what someone was doing, that these damning bits of numbers and letters had appeared on her screen completely by accident, that only through someone's extreme carelessness had it been transmitted to her computer. That if anyone realized what they had done . . .

It took her an hour and a half to follow the trail, to get through the barriers and the traps, and bring the complete formula to her screen. It was there, all of it. It was called Red Ribbon, and it had been developed at the research center – by her own people, right under her very nose. While she was feeling sorry for herself, letting the world go by, they were giving birth to this monstrous thing, this molecular chain of horror that could kill every form of life on earth if it was ever released from its viral cage.

She sat back, let her breath come in slow, easy measures. They had been thorough, very complete. She had taught most of them their craft, and she had taught them well too. They had Red Ribbon and they had an antidote for it too. An antidote! If the whole thing wasn't so grim she'd have to laugh at that. She could imagine the list, something with a security classification as high as Red Ribbon itself – who's on the list, who gets the shots and who gets left out. Now that'd be something to see. She knew who wasn't on the list, whose name she wouldn't find: Dr. Corrina Devonshire. Wups! Sorry, Corrina, guess we missed you somehow.

She set the .45 aside. She wasn't going to kill herself now, she had other things to do. She still didn't have a reason to live. But now she had a reason not to die . . .

Twenty-nine

"Up there," Corrina said, leaning forward and pointing past the dash, "what's that, what are they doing up there?"

"Said there was a toll, right?" Barb said.

"Yes, you did, but . . ."

"That's called a toll booth, doctor. And those bozos are toll collectors. Nice, huh?"

"Jesus," Axel said to himself.

Forty or fifty rusted cars formed a wall across the road head, one crushed relic piled atop the next. The line started twenty yards on either side of the road itself. Blocking the way through this mess was a semi with armor plate welded to its sides. It was totally illegal, of course – past the point of UN protection, not close enough to any army's lines. You didn't *have* to pay – if you could get past those gorillas, smash through the semi, the toll was absolutely free.

Axel recognized the toll collectors at once. In the war-torn cities of the nation they were an all too common sight. Mercenaries, misfits and a sprinkling of deserters from both sides – goons who worked strictly for pay and had no allegiance to anyone except themselves.

"The other side of the roadblock is the Unoccupied Zone," Barb said. "The airport's there – all we have to do is get past these characters."

Axel looked at the goons. They were all well armed. Most of them looked like they'd rather shoot than let anybody through.

"Why do I get the idea we're not talking your ordinary toll booth here? I don't think these clowns are looking for pocket change."

"Real astute, Axel. I think you've got something there."

Corrina frowned. "What are we supposed to do? Do they tell us what to pay? We can't afford a great deal."

Barb gave her a look and shook her head. She pulled the van off the road, stopped and folded her arms. "Time, anyone? Who's got a watch that works?"

"Six forty-eight," Axel said.

"That's about right."

"About right for what?"

"Sundown. Nighty-night time."

"So now we do what?"

"Now we wait."

"What about the toll?"

"It's taken care of, Axel. Relax, okay? Don't worry about it."

"Huh-uh, that won't cut it, Barb." Axel sat straight and faced her. "Damn it, you're doing it again. Just charge right ahead, leave everyone else in the dark."

"Dark's what we're waitin' for, or close enough to it. Which is just about . . . now."

Barb grinned and slapped the dash. "There we go. The party's about to begin, folks."

Axel started to speak, then stopped. Leaning past Corrina, he could see them coming up in the big side mirror. At first there was a plume of road dust. Then a line of long, ancient Cadillacs roared up beside the black van, valves clacking, exhaust choking the air. All the Caddys were convertibles – they hadn't started out that way, but that's what they were now – and every car was packed, crammed with armed men, oversized hulks dressed in chrome and rusty tin, radiator armor, Michelin hats and thick Pirelli boots. They spilled out of the cars and glared at the toll collectors. The toll collectors glared back. Axel thought both sides looked alike.

Barb opened the driver's door, jammed a big pistol in her belt and stepped out.

"You two wait here. Don't go anywhere."

"Hold it right there." Axel grabbed her arm. "What's going on? Who are these clowns and what are they doing here?"

Barb jerked away. "This is our *escort*, Axel. Okay? You want to get out of Steel Harbor? This is how we get out."

Barb jumped to the ground. Axel nodded at Corrina and they followed Barb down.

"I don't like sitting and waiting when my hide's on the line," Axel said. "Kind of an old habit of mine."

Barb shrugged. "Suit yourself. Just stick with the van and don't get in the way."

"Axel's right," Corrina added. "I'm grateful, Miss Wire, but I don't intend to sit on the sidelines and – My God, what's *that*?"

Corrina stared. The metal-clad warriors spread out and gave way as a forklift whined through the dust. Big Fatso sprawled on his oversized sofa, Maxie Lou at his side.

"I don't like this very much," Corrina said.

"Christ, Barb, what is that – a man or a platoon?"

"You, and you –" Barb jabbed a finger at the pair. "Stay here. Stay on *this* side of the van. Do not follow me, do not interfere. Are we clear on this?"

"Shit." Barb didn't wait for an answer. She shook a strand of hair from her face and stalked off toward Big Fatso. Axel cursed under his breath, but stayed behind.

The forklift lowered Big Fatso close to ground level. Barb stopped ten yards away, hands on her hips.

"You're on time,"she said. "I admire that in a man."

Big Fatso grinned. "May I say you ah, look especially lovely today, Miss Wire? Quite fetching."

"Yeah, so do you. You got the money or not?"

Big Fatso looked crushed. "So pretty and so goddamn rude," he told Maxie. "Why can't ever'one be nice as me?"

"That'd be friggin' Paradise, hon. But it ain't going to happen in our time."

Barb rolled her eyes. "Are you clowns through? I've got a dog fight and a major accident after this."

"Be that way. See if I care." Fatso snapped his sausage fingers. One of the Junkmen stepped up with a briefcase. He walked over to Barb and opened it up.

Barb looked inside and made a face. There was nothing there but a single gold credit card.

"All right, what's this?" She held the card in two fingers and wrinkled up her nose. "I said *cash*, Fatso. You want me to spell it for those who don't know their letters yet? That's C . . . A . . . Damn it, you've done this before, what's the matter with you?"

Fatso spread his hands. "I had to work fast, Barb. You were the one said tonight, remember? Not me. That is a gold debit card, with seven-hundred-fifty thou credit on it. It's as good as cash."

"Wrong. Nothing's as good as cash."

"What am I going to do, stiff you?" Fatso didn't wait for an answer. "I've got a reputation to uphold in the bidness community. It's the best I could do on short notice. You want the deal, you don't want it, what?"

Barb worked her mouth like she'd tasted something bad.

"I don't like it, but I'm not going to stand around with a bunch of ugly guys all night. I'll do it."

"Fine, fine!" Fatso clapped his hands. "Now, I'd like to have those lenses."

Barb reached in her jacket and drew out a flat metal carton. She stepped closer to Fatso and opened the lid. The two blue lenses floated in a colorless sea.

"Excellent, all *right*!" Fatso beamed and reached out for his prize.

"No, no, you can't! *Please!*"

Barb drew back, turned and saw Corrina running toward her from the van, Axel at her heels. The flesh was stretched taut across Corrina's face, and her eyes were dark with rage.

"That – doesn't – belong to you! You don't have any *right*!"

Axel glared at Barb. "What the hell is this? I can't believe you'd –"

"Back *off*, Axel . . .!"

Three of Fatso's Junkmen were on Axel and

Corrina before they could take another step. Safeties went *snick-snick-snick!* and the two were looking down the ugly snouts of P-29s.

"Oh, now, ain't this a joy?" Big Fatso clapped again. "Axel Hood, Mr. Freedom Fighter, and the famous Cora D.. We can likely get autographs, Maxie Lou."

Axel's face was grim. "I don't – understand you. I thought I did but I don't. How can you do something like this?"

"You've never had a head for business, Axel. If you did, you wouldn't be in the baby-sitting trade."

A cry stuck in Corrina's throat. She came at Barb, both fists swinging. Axel reached out and pulled her back. Corrina jerked away, and tears of anger streaked her cheeks.

"I hope Charlie's watching this," Axel said. "Charlie'd be real proud."

"Charlie is *dead*. Remember?" Barb's eyes were cold as ice. "He is dead because he was fool enough to get mixed up with people like *her*. Just like you, Axel." She let out a breath. "Hell, you are wasting my time. Unless you and the lady can rake up more than seven-hundred-fifty big ones between you, Big Fatso's here's the highest bidder."

She turned and let her eyes sweep the crowd. "Do I hear Eight? Eight-fifty? Sold, to the large gentleman on the sofa."

Barb slipped the gold credit card into her pocket and handed the metal box to one of the Junkmen. The Junkman took it to Big Fatso at once. Fatso clutched it tight.

"I have said it before, Miss Wire, an' I'll say it

again. It's a genu-wine delight doin' bidness with you. I hope, in times to come –"

"Can it," Maxie said. "You ain't going to buy that toy so don't keep lookin' at it."

"I love it when you pout," Big Fatso told her. "I start gettin' all – you know . . ."

"You two can play footsie on your own time," Barb said. "We're not finished here yet. The rest of the deal still goes." She nodded toward the toll collectors lined up down the road. "Toll fee, full escort. Safe passages for us to the airport in the Zone."

"Well now . . ." Big Fatso looked thoughtful. "I don't know if we can manage that, Miss Wire."

"What?" Barb stepped forward. "Listen, friend –"

"No. You listen to me, Barb." Fatso's voice went flat. "There's been a slight change of plans, you might say. You and me ain't all that different in our thinking, if you know what I mean, both of us havin' our own well-being at heart an' all that."

Barb didn't breathe. Her fingers itched to go for the weapon in her belt, but she had more sense than that.

"Why don't you stop blabbin' and just say it, Fatso? I haven't got all day."

"Yeah, I bet you do, now." Fatso wagged a finger at her. "You want to make a guess? I bet you could get it first time. I was offered a better deal than yours, and I couldn't see no way to refuse."

"You son of a bitch."

"Well, yeah, you could have somethin' there."

Fatso raised a hand. A Junkman wearing rubber floormats and a car radio around his neck blew a loud blast on his whistle. Sirens began to wail. Barb jerked around, saw the lights begin to flash, saw the Steel

Harbor cops screech past the rusty wall of cars. Behind them came two heavy, armor-studded Congressional T-40s, modified mud-daubers with twin copper cannons and the new Rattler Twos.

Black-clad troopers spilled out of the armored cars, weapons at the ready. The local cops left their lights blinking, folded their arms and leaned against their hoods. This wasn't their show, but they wanted folks to know that they were there.

A big Congressional noncom with regulation hair stalked through his troopers with murder in his eyes. Behind him came Colonel Victor Pryzer, his uniform blacker than black, gold on his jacket, gold on his pants, gold everywhere. And, at his heels, was Steel Harbor Chief of Police Willis. Standing next to Pryzer, Willis looked as resplendent as a drowned sewer rat.

"I'll tell you what," Axel said, "you got to get up pretty early to get ahead of Barb Wire. Looks like someone did."

"Aw, shit," Barb said.

Me and Lutzo was with the 55th 'Murican Infantry for two, I dunno, three friggin' years. We was in that Powder River thing where ever'one got kilt or got their ass froze off. So what do they do? They give us a week of R&R and then toss us right in the middle of that Seattle shitstorm. That's where Lutzo got three of his fingers shot off. The medic says, "You shoot with left or your right, soldier?" Lutzo looks down and sees it's his right that's got the finger's blowed off, and says, "The right's the one I use, doc, the one that's got the finger's shot off." "Yeah, well you better start learning with your left hand now," the medic says. "Next!"

Lutzo, he is real pissed off about this. What does it take to get out of this mess, he's sayin', and that's what I'm sayin' too. A couple of minutes later, Lutzo points at the ditch off the road and says, "There, that's how you get out. There ain't any way but that." I see he's pointing at the stack of guys from our unit we was talking to at breakfast the day before. Now they're lyin' still and the flies are buzzin' round 'cause we're short of body bags. "That's it," Lutzo says, "you get out of this outfit you gotta be dead. That don't seem like a good idea to me." This same thought had crossed my mind before. Lutzo losin' some parts of hisself, and me giving strong consideration to parts *I* might be losing most any day now – put all that together, and Lutzo and me come to the same conclusion: We decided to un-join the US Army soon as it got to be dark.

They shoot you, of course, they catch you running off. Me and Lutzo seen 'em do it a couple of times. If we stayed, though, some Congressional trooper'd blow our heads off, so what the friggin' difference did it make? I couldn't see how we'd be less deader either way.

It was a good time to go 'cause we was marching our butts off south after the Congressionals had damn near run us in the ground. We was staggerin' down to Portland, looking more like a bunch of mangy dogs got loose from the pound than an army of any kind. There wasn't much food, and the officers and noncoms was hoarding most of that, so that's when me and Lutzo took off. Me and Lutzo, and about two hundred other ol' boys, which is 'bout how many was leaving every night.

Man, it felt good to be out of the army, I'll tell you what. Or it did for about the first hour and a half. After that it started pourin' down rain, and of course we'd left our friggin' packs behind 'cause we didn't want nothing to do with the army anymore. And that's where our ponchos and tents were, but we hadn't thought of that.

It rained for four days. We ate up the handful of rations we'd took the first day, and our bellies startin' aching real bad. There wasn't no place to get dry, so we mostly stayed wet. The fifth day the rain eased off and we found us a farm. There was smoke coming out of the chimney, and Lutzo and me had learned somethin' in the army, which was you didn't go runnin' in blind somewhere till you knew what you was running into.

There was four of 'em in there, huddled around the fireplace, havin' theirselves a time. "Sweet Jesus," Lutzo said, "you smell that? Those mothers has shot 'em a deer. They've killed a friggin' *deer*!" And sure enough they had. It was turning on a spit and its juice was drippin' down in the fire.

Well there wasn't anything we could do but what we did. Lutzo stayed at the window and I went round and kicked in the front door. We was both firin' full automatic and it didn't take a second and a half. Man, that meat was good. I don't think it was deer, what I think it was was a big friggin' dog. I didn't see no reason to tell Lutzo that, he had his heart set on deer.

While we was haulin' those boys out back, I saw they were wearing that Armored Division patch – the one with the treads and the friggin' happy face. "Damn sons of bitches," Lutzo said, "if they'd been infantry they'd of had someone on post. Serves the mothers right."

And that was true as it could be. You ought to listen good in training. You might learn somethin' that'd later save your life.

[Excerpt from *A Renegade Remembers*, T. R. Quinn, Blood River Press.]

- Johnny Gray Wolf, PhD, *Fall From Glory* (2032), University of the New Sioux Nation Press.

Thirty

Pryzer looked like he'd eaten a crate of canaries. He'd found this riding crop somewhere, and he walked around slow, slapping the stick along his thighs. He glanced at Axel and Corrina, took a lot longer looking Barb up and down, stripping her naked with his eyes, dressing her and stripping her again, thinking of all the really fun and nasty things he'd like to do, happy as a clam because now they weren't fantasies flitting through his head, now they were things he truly intended to do, when he and that overstuffed pirate got their business done.

Finally, Pryzer turned to Big Fatso, waiting long enough to let him know that he, Victor Pryzer, wasn't coming to *him*, that everyone should understand it was the other way around.

"Very nice job, Mr. Fatso. You're to be commended. Indeed, a fine piece of work if I do say so."

Fatso tossed his head and laughed. "You can keep the damn *commendin'*, Colonel, and I'll take the pay!"

He leaned his great bulk an inch forward, an inch and a half, an effort as great as the continental drift.

"You'll appreciate this, Barb – well, you won't really, I don't guess you'd go as far as that . . . Two mil for the lenses, okay?" He ticked off the numbers on his fingers. "A million dollar bounty on *your* head

– plus another mil for the lovely and famous doctor over there. And there's the seven-hundred-fifty thou you got in your pocket. I'll be takin' that back. Oh, the Lord has shined upon me. I am having a *very* good day . . ."

He nodded, and one of the Junkmen walked up to Barb, grinned and stuck his grubby hand in the pocket of her vest. Barb slapped it away, kneed the Junkman and punched him in the nose.

The Junkman groaned, went down and curled up on the ground. His buddies hooted and howled.

"No touching," Barb said. "Save the romance for your sister, pal."

She picked an imaginary speck of dust off her sleeve, frowned at it and blew it in the air.

"Marvelous, marvelous!" cried Fatso. "This is better 'n daytime TV!"

Three of Fatso's Junkmen came at Barb, weapons at the ready. Chief Willis stepped up in their path. "Beat it," he said, "I'm the law here."

The Junkmen glared but backed up.

"I'm sorry, Barb, I gotta take that weapon," Willis said.

"Go ahead. No one's stopping you."

Willis gently drew the pistol from her belt. He wouldn't meet her eyes. Barb thought he looked awful. It was clear he wasn't enjoying this at all, but she wasn't about to let him off the hook.

Colonel Pryzer stalked past Barb, gave Willis a fishy eye and stopped before Corrina. Corrina stood straight. She looked right through him, her gaze a thousand miles away.

"Amazing," Pryzer said. "The things they can do

210

these days. You don't look a thing like your picture. Prettier, I'd say, but you weren't a bad looker before."

He touched her shoulder with his riding crop, let it slide along her throat, up to the side of her cheek.

"The face can be deceiving, but the eyes, now the eyes don't ever lie, do they, Dr. Devonshire?"

Pryzer moved the riding crop down Corrina's neck, to the vee of her breasts. Corrina drew in a breath but didn't move.

"I'll tell you what," he said, "those deadbeats up in Washington have been having friggin' fits since you ran away. I can't tell you how eager they are to have you back.

"'Fore we do that, though I think I'll have to – show you just how eager we all really are." He leaned in close, and Corrina could smell his sour breath. "What do you think? You and me an' Barb Wire? Would that be somethin' or what?"

Corrina spat in his face. Pryzer's smile vanished. He carefully wiped his cheek with a folded napkin, wadded it up and dropped it to the ground. Then, with no warning at all, he whipped the riding crop viciously across Corrina's face.

Corrina cried out. A thin line of red striped her cheek. Axel went for Pryzer, coming in low, fists at his sides. One of Fatso's Junkmen took a step forward and rammed the butt of his rifle in Axel's belly. Axel went down. He shook his head and came up to his knees.

"All right, that's enough of that." Pryzer looked bored. "Do your duty, Chief Willis. Arrest 'em all. I'll want them at Interrogation in an hour. Not an hour and a *half*, Willis. Do you read me clear?"

Willis didn't move. "What's the charge, Colonel?"

"What? What? What did you say?"

"I said —"

"I *heard* what you said." The color rose to Pryzer's face. "Goddamn you, mister . . . Vagrancy. No visible means of support. Overparking. Crimes against the state. Get 'em *out* of here!"

Willis muttered under his breath. "All right, over there. Move it, Mister."

He pushed Axel roughly in the chest, jerked his thumb at Corrina and Barb. He motioned them back until they were flat against the side of Barb's van.

The Junkmen stood around and watched. They didn't see a lot of women like Barb and Corrina. In fact, no one even came close.

Willis turned on them and jabbed a finger in the air. "All of you bastards – outta here. This is police business. Move your shaggy butts!"

The Junkmen complained, turned and walked away.

"Hold 'em together," Willis told Axel. "Make it easy on yourself." He circled the cuffs on Axel's wrists, backed him against the van and moved on to Corrina. When he was done, he stepped behind Barb. Corrina gave Axel a puzzled look. Axel frowned at Willis, and Willis looked somewhere else.

"I'm sorry about Charlie, Barb. I had nothing to do with that. I don't know if it makes any difference or not, but I wanted you to know anyway."

Barb started to answer and stopped. She could feel his hands, feel the cold metal of the cuffs. What she couldn't feel, or hear, was the customary *Click*! when the cuffs snapped shut. More than that, she knew it wasn't standard procedure for the cops to slip a grenade in your hand. That wasn't normal. It hardly ever happened at all.

"I appreciate you saying so," Barb said. "And – I hope you've got a job offer somewhere else."

"I'm retiring," Willis said. "I haven't announced it yet."

"You're downright peculiar sometimes, Chief."

"You noticed, huh?"

Willis walked off. He nodded to a pair of Pryzer's Marines. "They're all yours," he said. "Good luck, boys."

The black-clad troopers gave Willis semi-snappy salutes. They looked at their Colonel, but Pryzer was talking to the fat guy on the forklift truck.

"You three," the one with the corporal's stripes said, "let's go."

"Where we goin, hon?" Barb gave him a lazy smile and wet her lips. "Mind if I bring this along?"

She brought the grenade from behind her back, and bounced it in her hand.

"Sh – shit!"

The corporal's face went white. The other Marine gripped his rifle, swept it around at Barb. Axel jerked the weapon from his hands, swung the barrel up and smashed his face. The corporal dropped his own weapon and ran. Corrina reached down, swept it up, squeezed the trigger and sprayed the area like a hose. The weapon shuddered in her hand, chewing up Marines, Junkmen and cops.

Pryzer turned and stared. "What the holy hell – !"

"Party time," Barb said under her breath. She grabbed the pin on the grenade, pressed down the

213

safety handle, drew back and lobbed the thing as high and as far as she could.

"Oh, my God . . ." Axel said.

Barb ran past him, threw herself into the driver's seat of the van. Axel shoved Corrina in, leaped up behind her, tried to close the door.

"Huh-uh, I'm not sticking around here!" Willis gripped the open door as the big engine roared into life, sprawled over Axel, driving Corrina into Barb Wire.

"Cool it," Barb yelled, "don't mess with the friggin' driver!"

Willis hung on, half in and half out, as Barb burned rubber and raced down the road. He felt as if he might be someone else, watching things happen that had nothing to do with him. The van was doing sixty, sixty-five, headed straight for the threatening barrier ahead. Yet time seemed to drag to a stop, nearly stand still. Back across the road behind the van, he could see a dark and deadly metal egg, falling, falling through its arc in the hot and syrupy air. Troopers and Junkmen fled in every direction, moving, in Willis's eyes, in agonizing slow motion, their bodies strained, faces twisted in fear. He watched as Pryzer dived for cover, his big thighs churning down the road.

Then he saw Big Fatso's face, saw the fat man had also followed the grenade along its path, watching it dropping now, taking a week, taking a week and a half before it landed in his lap. Big Fatso screamed, a heavy bass note that dropped into nowhere as Fatso's tape ran out . . .

Everything came back to life in Willis's head. It had been only four-point-seven-two seconds since Barb had tossed the grenade. Nice hang-time, Willis thought, as the world came apart, as Big Fatso, the lovely Maxie Lou, the oversized sofa and the forklift truck, vanished in a ball of phosphorescent white. Caddy parts and Junkmen merged into one as an orange fireball sucked itself high into the air.

"My God!" Axel blinked in awe. "That was a – that mother was a NAP-Time grenade!"

"What's that?" Willis asked.

"NAP-Time. Neutron Anti-Personnel device. US Army, TD-24. Where the hell did you get that thing? They're not even in production yet."

"I dunno." Willis shrugged. "Took it off a drunk, I guess. You'd be surprised. We get all kinds of weird stuff."

"Pipe down back there," Barb shouted, "we're going through right now!"

"We're – *what*?" Axel looked past Barb and went white. Corrina closed her eyes. Willis got a quick look at the speedometer: ninety, ninety-five . . .

The big armored semi loomed ahead. Toll guards let off a few rounds then ran for their lives.

"We're going to die – we're going to die!" Willis yelled.

Barb didn't answer. She crouched over the wheel, gripped it tight. The semi was massive, blocking out everything in sight. Barb held her course. Thirty yards, ten –

At the last possible instant, she veered sharply to the left, missed the semi by a foot and a half, and burst through the rusty wall of cars.

Metal shrieked, and jagged shards of steel ripped at the sides of the van. Something heavy struck the roof, cracked the armored glass and fell way. The van howled into the open, its armored hood battered but still intact.

Willis touched his face, stared at his hands. "I'm alive? My God, I'm still alive!"

"That could change any minute," Barb said. "Shut up. Axel, crawl back there and rack us out some weapons. No pea-shooters. Heavy stuff."

Axel nodded. He eased over the seat, rubbed his hands at the impressive inventory.

"Nice. Wish we'd had half this shit at Cripple Creek. We'd have made it out in one piece."

He picked out four of the black-snouted Laser-Chaser Tens, semi-As with the optional Screamer switch for that messy, close-up work. He grabbed four extra ammo slings, dropped an Australian Roo Revolve in each one, and added a couple of grenades.

"You been in police work long?" he asked Willis.

"Apparently long enough." He nodded at Barb. "Does she know what she's doing?"

"No, of course not."

"I heard that," Barb said. "Quit jawing back there."

"She hears what she wants to hear," Axel said. He passed two of the weapons up to Willis. "When she doesn't, she —"

"*Company! Hang on!*"

A shell burst in midair, twenty yards ahead of the van. Glass cracked. Something howled beneath the hood. Barb could feel the concussion in her belly. She jerked the wheel to the left, counted to three, steered to right again. Two more dirty wads of black exploded to the left. Shrapnel rattled against the van.

"They shot my rearview off," Barb said calmly. "There's a shooter hole in that rear wall. Shove the red doohickey right."

Axel held the sides of the van to stay on his feet. Willis was right behind him. Axel opened the narrow slit. He knew what he'd see, but the hair climbed the back of his neck anyway.

"Congressional T-40s. Double Rattler-Twos front-mounted. I can see the copper-barrels. Those damn things are faster than I thought. Three of your cop cars are dragging ass in the rear."

"Not my cop cars," Willis said. "I don't work there anymore."

"I stand corrected. And let me say I feel your decision was well timed."

"I thought so. A moment appears when you tell yourself your lifestyle's not working out. You have to know exactly when that moment is. A second too soon, a second too late –"

Axel saw the flash from the long twin barrels of the nearest T-40s. He knew, from experience, what a flash looked like going somewhere else and what it looked like coming down your nose . . .

"Incoming!" he shouted, and hit the floor of the van.

The shell screamed like a tortured cat, exploded no more than ten feet above the van, ten to the right. Axel felt the shock, fought to draw breath, felt blood in his ears, blinked and saw Willis floating just above, saw to his surprise that he was floating too.

This is not right . . . floating's not good . . .

Willis let out a frightened yell.

Corrina screamed.

Axel slammed against the bottom of the van. Being weightless was no longer a problem. His back hurt, his legs were numb. Barb was shouting something he couldn't hear. It took him a moment to realize what had happened, why the dust and debris were still floating in the air. The shell-burst had lifted the van off the ground, flipped it completely over and set it back on its wheels again.

Barb was cursing, pounding on the dash. The van's engine sputtered, died, caught again and sputtered.

"For God's sake, get us out of here!" Willis yelled.

"I'm trying, damn it, just take it easy back there!"

"Oh, shit . . ." Willis grabbed Axel's shoulder and pointed a shaky finger past the van's rear window.

Axel looked. He thought he ought to panic, throw up or pass out. Instead, he just stood there and watched, knowing there was nothing he could do. More T-40s had appeared. Now there were six. The two directly behind them, and two on either side, all of them closing fast.

He watched, detached, as calm as he'd ever been in his life. It would take maybe two, three seconds before all the guns fired at once, scarcely time to review the events of his life, which hadn't been all that terrific, anyway, so why the hell bother about it now?

Bein' on your own ain't all it's cut out to be, which is somethin' me and Lutzo found out. You can do whatever you want and get up anytime, and there's no friggin' officers or sergeants telling you what to do next. The other thing is, you got to find all your own rations and somewhere to sleep and sometimes that's a hassle and a half.

Like, when we first de-enlisted from the 55th, you know, and come across those clowns from the Armored Division and kinda borrowed their supper and a place to spend the night. That's fine, except then you gotta figure out what you're going to do the *next* day, an' the day after that. We was right lucky at first, because a lot of the guys that was desertin' was going southeast of Portland, into the Cascade Mountains, where most of 'em got lost or starved to death or both. Me and Lutzo took off west, down past Salem and Eugene and over to the coast. There was more people there, but the war hadn't hit 'em so hard, and it was easier to steal a meal – or if the folks didn't want to cooperate, set their place afire an' drive them out. There's sometimes you got to do that.

About two months later we was down in California in the Sacramento Valley. That's where we first come on to Morgan Fritz. Fritz was runnin' the tollbooth scam south of Red Bluff on Highway 5. We'd run across similar operations twice in Oregon, but the bozos workin' 'em didn't have the weapons

219

and the men, and no one paid them any mind.

Morgan Fritz, now, he knew what he was doing. That sumbitch had a car wall forty yards wide and close on to thirty men. Me and Lutzo got work real quick, 'cause they was always needing good shooters. You know, someone'd run off or get kilt when some clown would try an' break through. We'd always get 'em, of course, but sometimes they'd get a few of us too.

We got along real good with Fritz, and later in the year when he started franchisin' the tollbooth scam, me an' Lutzo got our own operation down near Coalinga, and another one over to Fresno. It wasn't but a year after that before all the competition that could still run or crawl had hauled out, an' we was into Bakersfield and workin' the Barstow to Las Vegas run.

We might of expanded too quick, 'cause that operation nearly did us in. Mary Louise Gunn, who had all the illegal enterprise and black-market shit from Flagstaff down to Tuscon and on to El Paso and Rowell, she wanted to own *our* ass too.

That's what started the famous Toll Wars, which ended up with the Amarillo Massacre, and left me holding all the chips, and left Lutzo and the Big Bitch herself flat dead. I had the whole shootin' match then, or damn near, including the operations in Detroit, Toledo and the big mother of 'em all, Steel

Harbor. I figured, if me an' Morgan Fritz could get together on a deal, and R. J. Pine in Baton Rouge had a accident of some kind, we could bring the whole thing in line.

Damn, if this ain't a great country, I'll tell you what. And God bless the friggin' war . . .

[Excerpt from *A Renegade Remembers*, T. R. Quinn, Blood River Press.]

– Johnny Gray Wolf, PhD, *Fall From Glory* (2032),
University of the New Sioux Nation Press.

Thirty-one

Axel saw the white puffs of smoke, the yellow balls of flame, and he knew every one of the big T-40s had opened fire at once.

Auto fire . . . central targeting device . . . every god-damn shell lands at a single point of impact . . .

Axel hugged the deck, counted in his head . . .

Four –

    Three –

        Two —

Barb veered sharply to the right, two wheels down, two in the air. Someone cursed, someone yelled, Axel couldn't tell who.

A dozen shells exploded in a blinding flare of light. The road disappeared where the van had been seconds before. Concussion shook the earth. A wall of heated air struck the van, lifted it off the road, slammed it down again. Axel covered his face, bounced off the wall.

Up front, Barb fought for control, did a dizzy one-eighty, got the van going reasonably straight again.

"Great – driving," Axel told her. The words were dry in his throat. "After the war, you might think about the Demolition Derby. It's easier than this, and the pay's real good."

"Thanks. That's what I need, Axel. Career advice from you."

"Listen," Willis said, "those bastards are going to hit us again, you know that. I'd say next time they fire, you go *right*. That's what you did last time, so they'll thing you're going *left* this time, only you go *right* again. They'll think . . . Uh, wait a minute, shit, what if *they* think that *you'll* think –"

"Sit down somewhere, Willis, before I toss you out the back."

"I am trying to help, Barb. That's all. Trying to do me part."

"Yeah. That's what I was afraid of. Sit *down*, Willis!"

Willis sat.

Axel pressed his face to the narrow slot in the back. "They're closing up, forming on the leader. That son of a bitch Pryzer, no doubt. They – Damn, they're going into half-turn now."

"What's that supposed to mean?"

"New firing position. I'm guessing they won't drop their eggs on one point this time. Their computer'll work out a scatter-fire."

Barb made a rude noise in her throat. "Computers are basically stupid. The day I can't outdrive a dumb machine . . ."

"They won't let us get to the airport, will they? We'll never get out of here." Corrina gave Barb an icy look. "I don't suppose it matters, does it? Since I have no way to get into Canada anymore."

"Don't complain, lady," Barb told her. "Your lovely ass is still intact. You might want to think about that."

"*Incoming!*" Axel yelled.

"Wonderful." Barb gripped the wheel. "Hold on,

everybody." Axel braced himself for another back-breaking curve. He knew it didn't matter, whatever Barb thought about dumb machines. Left, right, straight up – the gunners back there were wise to her now. No matter what she tried, they –

The heavy tires howled. Powerful brakes caught, the van turned around twice, jolted to a stop. Shells screamed overhead. A dozen plumes of dirt and fire formed a deadly circle around the van.

Axel shook his head in wonder. *Any* direction was a disaster. The Congressionals had covered everything – everything except the insane, unreasonable act of coming to a complete and total stop under enemy fire.

Barb burned rubber, wrenched the wheel and left the road behind.

"What – where are we going?" Willis gripped the back of Barb's seat. "You can't outrun those things off the road. Those mothers are built for this terrain!"

"I can't outrun 'em anywhere. I've got to out-*think* them, Chief."

"Oh, well fine."

"God, over there!" Corrina jabbed a finger past Barb's face.

Barb saw them – two Steel Harbor police cars had left the pack. They were churning up dirt on the ruined plain, circling to the left to cut them off, drive them back toward the Congressional tanks.

"Willis, Axel – you see the red boxes back there? Two of them on the rear wall. Open them up. Hurry!"

Axel found them. They looked like oversized fuse boxes. He flipped up the covers. There were two sets of grips, two triggers.

"Okay, we got it," he called to the front.

"I'm turning away. When the ass-end of the van is in line with those mothers, let 'em have it."

"Uh, let 'em have what, Barb?"

"What do you care? *Do* it!"

Barb jerked the van into a sharp turn. Axel wasn't ready. He slammed into the wall, driving Willis to the floor.

"Don't you ever tell anybody what the hell you're going to do?" he shouted. "We can't read your mind back there!"

"Shut up. I'm in line . . . now. Hit the bastards. Hard!"

Axel looked at Willis. Willis gripped the trigger beside him.

"Do it," Axel said.

Thunder rolled through the back of the van. Axel could feel the shudder beneath his feet as seventy caliber lead rattled from under the armored floor.

My God, she's got fighter-plane weaponry down there . . . how did she get hold of that?

Tracers reached out into the growing dark. Axel caught a flash of yellow light, saw it brighten into a ball of white fire.

"Got him," he said, "we've got a confirmed back here."

One of the cop cars streaked across the flats, a burning comet of flame. The second car was too close. The driver cut frantically to his right, half a second late. A pyre of exploding gasoline rose up to the sky.

"Correction. That's two bogeys down."

Axel stole a glance at Willis. The men in those cars had been his men not fifteen minutes before. If the incident bothered him at all, it didn't show.

Axel checked out the T-40s again. Barb's off-road maneuver had forced them to change their tactics. They were coming together again, three on three, converging in a vee.

Axel leaned forward, his head close to Barb's. "Pryzer isn't going to stop, Barb. He'll run us right into the Unoccupied Zone, finish us off and work out the political problems after that. What the hell does he care?"

Barb forced a grin. "Colonel Pryzer's not going to play fair? That's hard to believe." She looked straight ahead. "I *know* what he's going to do. If we get out of this, we stop him first. That's the only way. That's it."

"Fine. How do we manage that?"

"In – in – whatever you said!" Willis shouted.

"Incoming?"

"Yeah, that's it!"

Axel didn't have to look this time. He'd heard that terrible banshee wail before. *Rockets!* XT-100s, most likely. Hand-held, loaded with high-explosive warheads and a phosphorous kicker. They were firing them off the tops of the T-40s. Three tubes per launcher, six vehicles . . .

"Here we go again, gang." Barb twisted the van through a dizzy, gut-wrenching course. The rockets blossomed around them, spewing hot and deadly petals of orange and white. Barb drove the van directly through a fireball. Axel closed his eyes, felt the raging heat.

"Okay, let's get a little confusion going here," Barb muttered to herself. She fumbled beneath the dash, found a black lever and pulled it straight out.

"Oh, Jesus, we're on fire," Willis said. "Purple stuff's coming out of the rear!"

"Good. That's what it's supposed to do. Axel, get up here and take the wheel."

"What?"

"Damn it, do you *always* have to argue with me? Do it!"

Axel crawled clumsily over the seat. Corrina looked at him and frowned. Barb gave him a wink, and slid back to the rear.

"You run into an emergency or anything," she said, "just yank that yellow switch."

"What for? Barb, where the hell are you going?"

Barb didn't answer. She shoved Willis aside, stopped at the arms rack, slung a Laser-Chaser Ten across her shoulder and picked up a satchel of Go-Go grenades.

Opposite the weapons rack was a wide, closed cabinet, built into the wall. Barb loosed a catch and the front of the cabinet whirred up into the wall.

Willis stared. "What's that? You're not going to . . . oh, shit, Barb –"

"Out of my way, Chief."

Barb stretched a long leg over the saddle of the black bike. It was very much like the heavy hog she'd ridden through the streets a few nights before. Charlie had built this one from scratch, too, and added a few features he'd never gotten around to installing on the street machine.

Placing a black helmet on her head, Barb kicked the machine into life. Its gut-throbbing roar filled the van. She clicked a switch on her handlebars, and the rear door of the van sprang open wide. Barb pulled down her visor, bent over the dash and jerked the throttle hard.

The black and chrome machine leaped out of the door, vanished in a cloud of the van's purple smoke . . .

She skirted the edge of the heavy veil, keeping just inside her cover. On the inner face of her visor, the radar projection showed six green blips past the smoke – two on the left, the others on the right. The smoke had a metallic additive that was supposed to act as an anti-radar element, but Barb didn't have a lot of faith in that. One of the basic rules of life was that things that were supposed to work didn't, half the time.

If I can see them, those suckers can probably see me as well . . . Okay, to hell with it – nobody gets out of this friggin' world alive . . .

Barb squeezed the handlebars, cut sharply to her right. The two T-40s on her left were maybe thirty yards apart, still heading toward the van. The four on the right had slowed down to half-speed and were bunched up tight. Maybe they were talking things over, she decided. Maybe they'd stop to have a beer.

Not a good idea, guys . . . gotta keep movin' out here . . .

She roared out of the purple cloud, straight for the four black tanks. Barb heard radio static in her ears, saw machine guns start to work. She hunched over the bike, kept her course right ahead. Bullets spouted geysers in her path. She wrenched the bike in a turn that plumed dirt in the air, brought her inches from the ground, whipped past the T-40s so close she could smell the fuel oil, the overheated paint. The gunners tried to reach her, but she was much too close, right under their noses, and the lead whistled over her head.

Do it – do it – do it – do it NOW, girl, or you're flat-ass dead!

Reaching blindly into her satchel, she clutched a Go-Go grenade in her fist, tore off the safety tab, tossed the silver ball across her shoulder. Reached in and grabbed another, tossed it after the first. Two grenades, for four tanks, was maybe overkill, she thought, but what the hell – grenades came cheap if you stole them from somebody else.

Barb twisted the throttle as far as it would go. The bike chewed dirt as she turned into the wide arc of a circle, away from the tanks, back the way she'd come . . .

Behind her, in the air, the Go-gos split open, the two halves of the sphere spinning away. Inside was a sleek, black and yellow dart, striped like a wasp and the size of a thick cigar. A micro video monitor went BEEP! *Tiny wasp wings flicked into place, pinhead retros whined. The Go-Go was the two-hundred-seventy-eighth generation of SMART missile-grenades – smart, in the sense that there was one thing they knew how to do: they could whine and whir and beep until they found a mass of metal with the proper weight and heat. They could send that information to a minuscule computer the size of a beetle's eye, which would then decide if this was a proper target, the right configuration, plus three-hundred ninety-six other bits of data, some of which were vital, some which weren't at all.*

All of this took less than one ten thousandth of a second after cover separation – a little too slow, but if the war lasted long enough some clever guy in RES/ WEAP would bring that number down . . .

Two of the four T-40s had their screens off. There was no excuse for this, any more than there was for slowing down, and no one would ever know why these incidents had occurred. The operator in the fourth tank had time to feel a chill at the base of his neck, had time to yell something like "SMART grenade coming in! SMAR –"

The two grenades exploded three-point-seven inches from their targets. The armor on the four vehicles turned white hot, but held – absorbed a great deal of the blast. Not enough, however, to keep the men inside from catching fire at once, and turning crispy black.

Colonel Victor Pryzer saw it all on his screen, saw what had happened, guessed what would happen next. He wasted half a second cursing the fools who had let that long-legged wild woman fake them out, then turned, grabbed the mike from his driver, a sergeant who was staring at the screen with his jaw hanging open.

"Number Two, get after her – burn that bitch!" He threw the mike at the steel wall. "Sergeant, we are pursuing that van, I believe. Would you kindly get on with that?"

"Sir – yes, sir!"

The sergeant swallowed hard, slammed the T-40 into high, and took off with a shudder and a roar. He didn't look at his colonel in the eye. He knew what

Pryzer had done, that he'd ordered the other T-40 to peel off after the motorcycle, to keep the biker off *his* back for a while. The men in the other tanks, and in Number Two, were good friends, and he didn't want the colonel to see the shame he felt, the relief that it was the other guys who'd gotten fried and not him.

Barb didn't take the bait. She knew Pryzer had to be in the tank that had hauled off after Axel and the others. She tossed her last Go-Go in the air, didn't bother to watch as it dropped its silver hide and buzzed toward Colonel Pryzer's sacrificial lamb. She didn't look back, but she heard the sound of thunder, saw the high reflection of death in the clouds overhead.

"There, that's it." Willis pointed to the low horizon. "You can see the lights of a plane coming in. The airport's just to the left."

Axel strained against the dark. "Two, three miles . . ."

"Closer to three. The harbor's on the right. You could smell it if you had the window down. Don't. Dockyards on the left, or where they used to be. Everything's turned to shit. Go straight half a mile, swing back off the flats and you'll find the main road again."

Axel bit his lip. "There's a lot of noise back there, and I'm thinking Barb's in the middle of it."

Willis looked alarmed. "*Barb* can take care of herself. She'll be here."

"You have all the confidence in the world, right?"

"Hey . . ." Willis spread his hands. "What are you trying to say, pal? My God, if I thought Barb needed help, I'd – I'd tell you to turn this van around right now."

"I think she needs help."

"Give her another minute. Give her a minute and a *half*."

Axel gave him a look, faced the front again, spotted the continuation of the road where Willis said it would be. He veered the van back to the relatively smooth surface, glanced at his watch.

"How much time have we got?" Corrina asked.

"We're fine. I think. That's probably the Canada flight Willis saw coming in."

"That's not an answer, Axel."

"I don't know *exactly* how much, Corrina. My watch is acting up, okay? All that shellshock's bad for people and machines . . ."

"There's nothing wrong with your watch." She reached for his wrist, caught his expression and backed off. The look in his eyes startled her, and frightened her as well.

"I guess I – don't have to know, do I? I keep forgetting I don't have any reason to hurry anymore."

Axel didn't look at her. "You've got a reason to stay alive."

"Do I? And what would that reason be, Axel?"

"For God's sake, Corrina –"

"What's that – look!" Willis squeezed her shoulder. "Up there, up ahead."

Axel squinted into the dark. He'd been driving without lights, and now he quickly flipped them on and off again.

"Oh, Lord!" Corrina stiffened beside him. Willis let out a breath.

232

Axel saw it all in the short instant of light. The foul black water to the right, the abandoned dockyard on the left. And straight ahead, two – three giant cranes, their skeletal frames stark against the sky. Below them, blocking the road, the carcass of a bus, a relic, a dinosaur maybe fifty years old.

He muttered to himself, rammed the pedal to the floor, knew if he gave himself a second to think he'd turn back.

Willis stared. "What the hell are you doing? You can't drive through a – bus!"

"Uh-huh. Can't go around it, either."

"Aw, shit," Willis moaned, "I could've stayed on the force, put in my twenty years."

"You wouldn't be happy. Retirement is a pain in the ass. Hang on, everybody . . ."

Thirty-two

Axel flipped the lights on high. Half a dozen toll guards whipped their arms up to their eyes, like animals caught in the road. They weren't expecting trouble – everyone ran, no one tried to squeeze off a shot.

The bus loomed ahead, blocking out the night. Ten seconds, Axel thought, no more than that . . .

"Axel . . ." Corrina clenched her fists. "What – what Barb said, if there was a – an emergency?"

Axel looked blank.

"The yellow thing. Pull the goddamn *yellow* thing, Axel!"

"Right, right." Axel came to his senses, reached beneath the dash, grabbed whatever he could find, nearly yanked the lever out by its roots.

A frightening sound shrieked up the scale, then blinding light flared on either side of the van. The van shook, bounced off the ground, and rockets the size of broomsticks whined into the dark.

"Look out!" Willis yelled.

Axel saw the rockets meet, converge in a perfect vee at the center of the bus. The relic ripped itself in half in a blinding cone of light. Axel closed his eyes, gripped the wheel and didn't slow down. The van passed through the firestorm, through the thunder and the rattle of glass and steel.

The giant, rusted cranes formed a tunnel of tangled metal, a narrow and treacherous path.

"Slow down!" Corrina yelled, digging her nails in his arm. "For God's sake, you're going to kill us all!"

"*I'm* going to kill us all?" He didn't take his eyes off the road. "I didn't put the goddamn bus on the road, I didn't –"

"Company," Willis said from the rear of the van. "One of the T-40s, comin' in fast!"

"Just one?"

"One's all I've got so far."

"Pryzer," Axel said under his breath. "Got to be. Any sign of Barb?"

"No, huh-unh, I can't see her, I – Wait, yeah, it's *her*!" He let out a yell. "She's right on Pryzer's tail. Jesus, she's doing wheelies!"

"Figures. The woman's crazy. Always has been. What's she doing now?"

"Can't see her. Too much smoke. Okay, there she is, she's right by the – oh, shit!"

Machine gun fire rattled against the rear of the van. Corrina covered her ears and buried her head. The sound drove Axel nuts. He felt like he was stuffed in a garbage can and every kid in the neighborhood was pelting him with rocks.

The armor-plate's good, but how good? If Pryzer keeps hitting us like that . . .

"Axel – !"

Corrina cried out, too late. Axel saw them in the glare of the lights – the road ahead was filled with Puncher Nines, the spike traps both sides used to screw up enemy traffic. The van was going eight-five. Half a second later all the tires exploded at once.

He jammed his foot against the floor – it was a useless, automatic gesture, he knew it wouldn't help at all. He opened his mouth to warn Corrina and Willis, saw Corrina's eyes go wide, felt the van swerve in a sickening motion to the left, felt the spine-wrenching jerk as it flipped on its side, skidded down the road in a shower of sparks . . .

The headlights exploded . . . he tried to find Corrina in the dark . . . Willis hurled past him, slammed into the windshield, kicked and struck Axel in the head . . .

It'll stop . . . passenger door's on top now . . . we can get out there . . . we'll be all right . . . gotta be . . . all right . . .

And that was the moment when a ragged hole opened in the night and Axel Hood fell in . . .

"Oh God, *no!*"

Barb jammed on the brakes, wrenched the bike to a stop, watched in horror as all the tires on the van went up in a puff of smoke, watched it flip over and spark down the street. She held her breath, certain for an instant Pryzer's driver would veer the T-40 aside in time . . .

The heavy armored vehicle plowed straight into the van's belly. Metal shrieked, a tire rolled dizzily down the road.

Barb raced her bike through the debris, screeched to a halt. The van's armored glass was spidered, she couldn't see inside. Raising the butt of her rifle, she smashed her way in.

Axel looked up, gave her a weary grin. A thin line of red trickled down his face.

"Nice car. Needs a little work."

"Right. So do you."

She reached inside, helped him sit up. Axel waved her off. Corrina was conscious. One of her eyes was black. He lifted her up to Barb, and went back for Willis.

"Aw, shit, man . . ." He thought Willis was dead. He was sprawled on his back, eyes wide open, staring at the wall.

"Don't move, he said. "Everything's broken. I'm done, I'm all torn up inside."

"Yeah, well, we don't have time for any of that."

Axel grabbed him by the shoulders, dragged him over the front seat and past the shattered glass.

Willis protested, tried to shake him off. Axel stood him roughly on his feet.

"We've got to move fast." Barb jacked a shell into the chamber of her weapon. She walked backwards, watching the T-40. A thin coil of smoke was rising from a vent.

"Willis – get 'em out of here. You know the way to the airport. It's just down the road. I'll stall these mothers, catch up with you there."

"Huh-unh. No way, Barb." Axel started toward her. Barb jerked around to face him.

"I'll meet you at the plane, Axel. I promise."

He looked at her, tried to read the meaning in he eyes, see what was hidden there.

"I'll meet you . . . I promise . . ."

They were his words, his promise, when he'd stayed behind in Seattle.

"I don't want to do this," he told her. "Not any-more."

"That doesn't matter much, does it?" She drew in a breath. "Get her out of here. Get her to the airfield. I'll *be* there, all right?"

"Barb –"

"We don't have time for this." She looked at him, turned away. "Goodbye, Axel."

She left him, made her way toward the T-40. Watched, listened. Axel hesitated, then ran to catch up with Willis and Corrina . . .

What the hell are you doing in there . . . I know you bastards aren't dead . . . I couldn't be lucky as that . . .

She walked her way carefully around the T-40, keeping well in shadow. Oil dripped on the road. She heard a faint sizzle, smelled burning wire.

Command hatch on top, one in the back . . . where else, can't be anywhere else . . .

She heard it, then, an almost imperceptible sound, the scrape of a boot on metal, leather touching steel –

The muzzle blast blinded her; she felt the hot lead hum past her cheek. She shot from the hip, sprayed a wide arc, watched her own copper noses spatter against the tank.

A trooper cried out in pain. His gun clattered to the ground. Barb kicked her bike into life, weapon still blazing, spun around a hundred and eight degrees, fired a burst again, saw three shadows spill out into the night, saw the empty bolt-hole, the round lid hanging down. Loosed a few rounds, knew she was a second too late.

Damn – they've got a hatch under *the thing . . . how was I supposed to know that?*

One down, then, three on the loose. And one of them had to be Pryzer; the colonel was too smart to stick his nose out first.

She cut the engine and drifted under cover of a large derelict warehouse, cursed her back luck. Catching them all in their tin can was too much to ask, right? Now all the rats were out of their holes and on the loose and she'd have to run them down. That wasn't fun. That was bloody *work*.

The moon came from behind dirty clouds, cast shadows of the twisted derricks in a checkerboard pattern on the ground. Barb watched from the warehouse wall. Nothing. Three minutes, four. A piece on the checkerboard moved, scuttered sideways like a crab toward the dark riverside.

That's not exactly the way out, pal. You don't much want to jump in that . . .

He crouched near the shore, clutching a rifle in his hand, looking out over the water. What for? What did he think he was going to do? Again, she knew it wasn't Pryzer. Pryzer was smarter than that.

The man was a perfect target. No way to miss. And that was the whole point, she decided. Drop one, the other two know where you are.

She took her eyes off the goon by the water, studied the dark around him. Looked back and saw that he was gone. She let out a breath. Pryzer had sent him there, of course. A decoy, a sacrifice to draw her out. What did Colonel Victor Pryzer of the Congressional Army care about another life? He'd sure lost count of the thousands he was responsible for.

Barb stepped off her bike and rolled it quietly

through the cavernous dark, avoiding the dim light from the network of beams open to the sky overhead. Her nerves were frayed raw; she jumped every time the wind rattled a broken pane of glass. Rats squealed, scampered across a floor littered with brittle paper, tin cans, the debris of the homeless men and women who had undoubtedly taken shelter here through the war. Barb tensed at every sound, felt her heart slam against her chest.

Easy, easy . .. you got the jumps, girl . . . calm down . .. or these bozos will do it for you . . .

She was careful to keep the bike's tires from running over paper, bits of broken glass. A tire made a distinctive sound, one that didn't belong to the night. Others were out there too, listening for anything unusual, anything out of place, just as she was herself . . .

Barb froze. Something moved outside, past the broken windows, moving quickly, back into the night.

She eased down the stand on her bike, left it there, checked the heavy weapon. Moving noiselessly to the window, she squinted out into the dark. Was it the same man, the one she'd seen by the river? Or another one, possibly Pryzer himself?

She waited, not daring to let out a breath, always looking straight ahead, letting her peripheral vision warn her of motion on either side.

Nothing.

There and then gone. She knew it was more than nerves. He'd *been* there, damn it, and now he was gone. Back to the river, or only a few feet away . . . right outside the building, crouching there, waiting for her to make a sound . . .

Don't move . . . wait . . . let him do it first . . . let him make the first mistake . . . and when he does –

The hairs climbed the back of her neck, crawled up her scalp.

He's not out there . . . he's in here . . . God, he's in here!

Barb heard his breath on the stock of his weapon, heard his fingers slide across the metal, threw herself to the ground. Rolled to the right, came up on her knees. Blinding light flashed in her eyes; lead chipped concrete exactly where she'd stood.

She didn't bring the weapon any higher than her waist. The Laser-Chaser thundered in her hands, kicked her in the belly, rattled all her teeth. She saw him go down, knew she'd nearly cut him in two, didn't wait to find out.

Running a crouch, both hands clutching her weapon, she made her way quickly to the bike.

No good to stick around now, get the hell out of here fast –

He hit her low, coming in from the left, buried his head in her belly, slammed her roughly to the ground. Barb felt the breath rush out of her lungs, heard her gun clatter across the floor.

The other one, you damn fool . . . the one from outside let you watch him while his buddy slipped in!

She felt his foul breath on her cheeks, smelled the stink of his unwashed hair. He straddled her, one hand on her throat, the other raised like a blade, ready to chop up beneath her nose, drive bone and cartilage into her brain . . .

One arm was twisted, caught beneath her back – she jerked up the other, caught the hard edge of his palm on her arm. She gasped, cried out against the pain as her arm went numb.

The man laughed, tossed her arm aside, slapped her hard on the face, slapped her again, and again . . .

Barb smelled her own blood, felt the darkness closing in, struggled to free her other arm. The goon had thought of that. He punished her hard, measuring the blows now, giving her time to think about what was coming next. With his free hand he let go of her throat, let his fingers snake down to her breasts. He was beating her to death, but that was no reason to deny a little pleasure along with the work itself . . .

She was almost under, the sounds of life fading in her head. Then the anger, the shudder of revulsion at his touch jerked her back, brought her to the surface again.

"Bastard! You *sorry* son of a bitch!"

She raised her useless arm, clawed desperately at his face. He cursed her, slapped her aside. She arched her back, brought all the muscles in her belly to play, drew her right leg up high and hooked it around his neck.

The goon blinked in surprise. He grabbed her leg with both hands, fought to break free. Barb gave a harsh yell, blew out all her breath, and wrenched him to his back. Her trapped arm was free. She raised it over her head, rammed her elbow once into his throat, heard everything crack, heard it all give way, knew that he was dead. Still, she hit him again, couldn't make herself stop until her energy was gone and her body went limp.

She'd lost control before – not often, once or twice. Now she felt the familiar mixed emotions of sheer exhilaration and shame. She'd heard soldiers talk about it – Axel, for one. It was something that happened. The best thing to do was not think about it at all.

Barb ran her fingers through her hair, stood, found her weapon and walked shakily to her bike. The place was getting crowded and noisy, time to bug out. Pryzer would have to be senile and deaf if he hadn't heard the gunfire, the wrestling match.

She rolled the bike around the far inside wall, keeping to the dark. The big open door, the way she'd come in, was a little too easy. Maybe there was another way, some place the homeless people had wrenched a tin panel aside –

"Hey, are we havin' fun or what!"

Barb froze, turned, saw Pryzer in the big doorway, a shadow against the greater dark. Light flared in his hand. A machine gun chattered. The man Barb had killed twisted, flailed its arms and legs as Pryzer slaughtered him over and over again.

He stopped suddenly, stalked over to the corpse, kicked it and cursed beneath his breath.

"Where the hell *are* you, Barb? You hiding somewhere?"

Pryzer laughed and sprayed lead wildly about the cavernous dark. Barb didn't move. She could raise her own weapon, get off a shot. If she missed, though, if he saw her . . .

"Don't you know we've got something heavy going, darling? You quit fighting me, you hear? I've got things to show you that you've never even thought about before!"

Nutso . . . flat out nutso, man . . .

Barb watched him, drew in a breath. He stood there, moving his head from side to side, sniffing the air, as if he might catch her scent in the dark. When he looked the other way, she rolled the bike forward as quietly as she could. When he turned back again, Barb stopped. He searched the night, looked right at her. Barb felt her skin crawl. He was ten yards away now, his weapon pointed right at her belly.

He stood there forever, pinning her in the dark. Finally, he turned, walked slowly backwards towards the door, his weapon sweeping form left to right.

Barb waited, watched his shadow stretch across the concrete floor, and disappear.

Where are you, Pryzer? Waitin' for me, right? Just standing there, hoping I'll do something dumb like ride out of here and let you blow my head off . . .

"Fine," she said under her breath, "you want it, you got it, pal."

She raised her boot and kicked the bike into action. The sudden sound fractured the silence, echoed off the tin walls. Barb squeezed the throttle up to a high, torturous roar, burned rubber, made a hard left and streaked out the open door . . .

I remember him because we found out we had the same birthday, although I was a year older than he was. Vic Pryzer was twenty-two and I was twenty-three. We were both working at KOLD-TOWN KOLOSSAL, which maybe no one remembers anymore. It was a long time ago before the war, but KOLD-TOWN was the biggest refrigerator outlet in the east at the time. I mean, it was Sale City every day – clowns, balloons, flags, you name it. Folks would come in and we'd get 'em worked up and we wouldn't let them *out*, you know? Buy a fridge or you don't get outta here, ma'am. We'd sell a fridge to some goof and his wife, they'd walk out of there in a daze – they already *had* a fridge at home, so now they've got two.

Anyway, that's how I met Vic. I was working sales on the floor on straight commission and pulling down a nice hunk of change, and Vic, Vic was doing the clown bit and making minimum wage – and he's afraid they're going to fire him from that. He says, "Hal, what is it, what am I doing wrong? I'm walking around looking dumb, what more do they want than that?" I tell him, "Vic, no offense, you got the floppy shoes, you got a polka-dot suit, a big nose. You *look* like a clown, Vic, but you're not *funny*, man. I mean, I don't think you *feel* like a clown inside. I think people see that. I think they see past the painted-on smile.

Vic, he looks at me kinda weird and says,

"I don't know what funny's *like*, Hal." And
he didn't, that's the thing. He didn't *get*
being a clown. He'd hop around in that
friggin' suit and give everyone the creeps.
This guy wasn't funny, he scared little kids.

I'm going with Marcie, a real cute girl who
worked upstairs in accounting, and we'd go
to a movie or a club sometimes. And
sometimes, *when* I'd leave after work with
Marcie, I'd see Vic Pryzer mooning around,
just watching, not doing anything, just
looking goofy and kinda lost like he did
sometimes. I knew he wanted to tell me
something, and he finally got around to it
after four or five weeks. What he wanted, he
wanted me to fix him up. See if Marcie had a
friend. God, I thought, the guy is going to
have a stroke just asking me about it. So
what was I going to do? Tell him I didn't
know any women who had a thing for
spooky clowns?

Marcie got Betticia who worked at the
desk next to hers, and I knew the minute Vic
saw her this was *not* a good idea. He turned
red and stumbled all over the place, and he
couldn't get a word out right. Marcie looked
at me, and Betticia looked like she might get
sick. It hit me right then, I thought, shit, I
can't believe this, but I do. This jerk's never
been with a girl, he's never had a date
before!

The whole evening was awful. I won't even
go into that. Vic didn't know what to do, he

didn't know what to say. If he had a chance to do something right, he did it wrong. It was like I've got two dates, and this six-year-old kid is tagging along.

We wound things up early, dropped Betticia off and then took Vic home. Then me and Marcie had a fight to end all fights, and she said she'd never speak to me again. She did, but she sure as hell meant it at the time.

The next day at work, the cops got to KOLD-TOWN KOLOSSAL right after ten, and by ten forty-five they had me and Marcie and Vic downtown. They talked my ear off for an hour and a half – what did we do the night before, where did we go and when? Everything everybody said, what happened after that.

They were especially interested in Vic, I got that right away. How long had I known him, what kind of guy he was. The stuff they were askin' scared the hell out of me, since it was pretty clear now it was just me and Marcie and Vic, that Betticia wasn't there . . .

Vic beat the trial. He had a good lawyer, and the DA didn't have a case at all. Vic still lived with his mother, and she swore up and down he'd never left the house after Marcie and me let him off. Betticia couldn't testify, of course. Christ, even if she'd known who she was anymore, you couldn't have brought her into court. Not the way she looked, not looking like that.

They told a lot of it at the trial, and they showed all the pictures around. Four of the jurors were so shaken up by the pictures they had to take 'em out. I wasn't supposed to see the pictures but I did. I can still see them in my head, and that was a lot of years ago. God, how could you ever even *think* about something like that? Much less doing it to somebody else . . .

I knew it was Vic. They couldn't prove it but I knew it was him. He and his mother left town right after that, which was a good idea for Vic. Someone would've killed him for sure if he'd been dumb enough to stick around.

I didn't hear his name again until the war. There wasn't a lot of stuff in the papers, of course, the Congressionals wouldn't let them do that. But word gets around. And when I heard some of the things they were doing to people, and that Victor Pryzer was in charge, I thought, damn, it started right there, didn't it, at KOLD-TOWN KOLOSSAL. With me and Marcie and Betticia that night. The three of us and Vic. Man, what an awful thing to happen. That crazy bastard had never been out with a girl, but he'd given 'em an awful lot of thought . . .

[Excerpt from the collection, *We Knew Them When*, C. J. Barnes, Privately Published.]

– Johnny Gray Wolf, PhD, *Fall From Glory* (2032),
University of the New Sioux Nation Press.

Thirty-three

Barb raced through the loading dock into the greater dark. Felt the hot, oppressive night. Smelled the foul odor of the harbor close by. She caught him at once in her lights, pinned him there, etched in a circle of searing white. He stood in the midst of the dockyard's rubble and debris, fifty yards away, forty-five . . . stood in a combat crouch, the machine gun gripped in his hands, a big man dressed in gold and black, his face dead-white in Barb's light.

Barb held her course, came right at him. She saw his red eyes, a wild creature caught in the road, saw his broad grin – a touch of joy there, hate, mad exhilaration, man whose soul was tainted red, a man whose only pleasure was pain.

Pryzer jerked his weapon up fast, fired a blast pointblank. Lead sang past Barb's head, thunked into armor, shattered her headlight. The Laser-Chaser bucked in one hand, slammed against her ribs. Pryzer blinked in surprise, danced as the copper glugs geysered at his feet.

Barb laughed aloud, shook her long hair in the breeze. Pryzer caught himself, stood his ground, squeezed off a burst of wild rounds. Barb skidded to her left, tossed a plume of dirt in her wake, and vanished behind a gutted truck.

Pryzer's bullets rattled off metal. Barb guided the

bike in a twisted course through the dockyard ruins, sometimes veering away from Pryzer's path, but always circling back.

He won't go far . . . he wants to finish me as much as I want to put an end to him . . .

Switching off the bike's power, she glided silently to a stop. Ahead was fifty feet of rusted steel plate, a high, haphazard wall nearly blocking out the night. It was the raw metal for the hulls of great ships that would never be built.

Barb rolled the big machine forward, then hesitated. Standing like a monstrous deck of cards on edge, the steel shafts offered good cover for a man in the dark, a man waiting for a kill. He could take a shot, vanish in the safety of a bulletproof maze, appear for an instant and disappear again.

She knew he was in there, sensed it, knew he had to be. If she'd found the place first she would have set up the ambush herself. Waiting him out was no good. Help would arrive for Pryzer, but no one was coming for her . . .

Quietly slipping off the bike, she rolled it back a safe thirty yards. Working quickly, she locked the handlebars – a mechanism Charlie had built in: if you were smart enough to steal Barb's bike, and get it started somehow, all you could do was drive it straight ahead.

With a small length of wire, she twisted a loop around the throttle control, left the loop loose, and rolled the bike back to the edge of the shadow-wall of steel. She stopped there, listened to the night. Nothing. But nothing was what she expected to hear.

Okay, Pryzer, you're the big-time shooter, take a shot at this . . .

Barb kicked the bike into life, shattering the silence. Holding the howling monster in check, she twisted the throttle wire tight, then let the bike go.

The big hog roared, leaped down the narrow way chewing up dust. Pryzer saw the beast coming at him. He didn't waste a second, didn't bother to look for a rider in the dark. Stepping from cover, he held the machine gun tight against his belly, filled the night with deadly fire. Lead spattered off the speeding bike, jerked it off the ground, shook it like a dog with a rat in its teeth, flipped it through the air.

Pryzer kept his finger on the trigger, threw back his head and laughed. He could picture the bloody image in his head, see the lead ripping through her flesh, see the pain, see the death . . .

Barb rolled for cover the instant she let the bike go, twisted once, landed on her belly, legs spread wide, elbows dug in the ground in a combat shooting stance, took a quick breath and let it out, laid down a killing blast of automatic fire . . .

Pryzer screamed, threw his weapon in the air. Barb saw him stumble, grab his thigh, stagger and run for the cover of the heavy plates of steel.

Barb cursed under her breath, came to her feet and followed him through the narrow way. The bike was silent now; Barb could smell gasoline, and prayed Pryzer hadn't hit the tank. Charlie's armor was good, but nothing held together if you hit it hard enough.

Quietly righting the bike, she ran her hands over every vital part in the dark, the way Charlie had taught her.

251

Check this and this and check that . . . you won't always have the light, little sister . . . learn to keep this mother working in the night . . . I do it, and so can you . . .

Barb swallowed hard, forcing him out of her head. No time for that now. Loosing the throttle wire, she rolled the machine out of the metal maze. Stopped. Listened. Moved ahead and stopped again.

For a while there was nothing at all. Then – *there!* She closed her eyes, cocked her head against the night. A boot. Stepping on glass. Then again. Nothing after that.

Keeping to cover, she edged closer to the sound. A warehouse. Much like the one where she'd encountered Pryzer and his goons, only this one stretched above the black river, close to the abandoned loading docks.

Barb paused to study the building's silhouette against the night. It was half in ruin, like everything else along the harbor. Three stories high in places, the walls still intact. Then, a few yards away, the roof would suddenly sag to the ground. There were ramps, stairways, leading up and down, some going nowhere at all.

She felt her heart beating against her chest, was certain Pryzer could hear it too.

He's up there, you know damn well he is . . . if you want him, you'll have to go and get him . . . the man isn't coming down here, he's not going t –

She saw the bright flash too late, felt the heat burn a furrow in the flesh of her arm. She fired a shot back, saw him duck into shadow above her, two stories high, back the bike into cover. He'd lost the machine-

252

gun back at the maze, but he still had a pistol. A Super-Nine from the sound. What – fifteen rounds? He wouldn't likely have an extra magazine. She'd hit him back there, but no way to tell how hard.

Barb kicked the bike into life, shot out of cover and up the steep ramp, hoped it didn't drop off into nowhere up there . . .

The half-rotten planks sounded hollow beneath her wheels, a sound that didn't comfort her at all. She paused at the top of the ramp, where Pryzer had disappeared. From there, the rampway led down. She leaned forward, peering into the dark. She could see where the roof had caved in, leaving skeletal beams sagging to the floor. Water dripped somewhere.

She saw him, then, on the rampway just below her own. She brought the weapon to her shoulder, squeezed off three quick shots. Pryzer ran, ducked beneath a crumbling wall. Barb roared down the ramp on to the littered floor, skidded in a tight, jarring turn. He was right there in front of her, staring at her. He opened his mouth and yelled, snapped off a wild shot and ran.

Barb heard him crash through debris, stumble, pick himself up again. She stopped for a moment to listen. Sound played tricks in the hollow, gutted building. Noises came from everywhere. Pryzer or a rat? Which way, right or left?

Left. Bootsteps on metal stairs, a sharp, distinctive sound, no mistaking that. She squeezed the throttle, jerked the bike around hard, roared through the dark.

Pryzer saw her, fired off a shot. He was halfway up the metal stairs. His features were twisted in anger, his eyes wide with pain. Barb caught a quick glimpse of a bloody rag wrapped around his thigh. He brought his arm straight out, looked down at her, squeezed the trigger, fired right into her face, fired again and again.

Barb kept coming, gauged her angle and her speed, suddenly veered the bike a good forty-five degrees, skidded to a stop. Raised the Laser-Chaser Ten to her hip, squeezed off five quick shots.

Victor Pryzer opened his mouth, gulping air like a fish to get the words out. The pistol dropped from his hand, clattered to the floor. He flailed his arms wildly about, a man who desperately wanted to fly, slowly fell backwards and disappeared.

Barb let out a shaky breath. She listened for a moment, then racked the weapon in the holster slung around her back. She didn't take her eyes off the spot above where Pryzer had stood.

"That's for Charlie," she said aloud. "Go straight to hell, you son of a bitch . . ."

She suddenly felt tired, heavy, everything hurt. She ran a hand through her hair, felt the tangles and the dirt. How long had it been since she'd left the others on the road, rooted Pryzer and his men out of the tank? It couldn't have been half an hour, less than that. It only seemed like a year.

They'll be at the airport now . . . got to get there, see Axel . . . there are things we've got to say, things that won't keep anymore, words that have waited too long . . .

Barb froze, jerked around. Heard the high, never-shattering shriek, saw the tin wall rip open, tear itself apart like a used paper shack. A cloud of choking dust rolled on to the loading dock floor. Something enormous burst through the cloud. Barb stared. A heavy-duty forklift, tall as a semi, thundered right at her, determined to run her down.

She desperately tried to back the bike free, out of the monster's path. There was no time, not half a second, nothing left at all. The rusty prongs of the forklift speared a wheel, skewered the bike and jerked it off the ground.

Barb yelled, kicked her leg up high to keep from losing a foot. She held on for dear life as the giant machine rolled crazily across the warehouse floor. Arching her back, she leaned out and looked straight up. High above in the driver's seat, Pryzer grinned at her like a lunatic. He held something out the window, waving it like a flag. Barb saw it was a bullet-proof vest. There were five copper slugs flattened on the upper chest. None were more than half an inch apart.

Nice pattern, she thought, *for all the friggin' good it did . . .*

The bullet-ridden vest flew past her in the dark. Barb tried to reach her weapon, but it was all she could do to hold on.

The forklift whined into a higher gear. She crawled off the seat, tried to climb clear. Pryzer gave a loud hoot, slammed straight into an abandoned car. Barb yelled and grabbed desperately for a solid hold. The forklift took off with a jerk, the derelict car crammed tight against Barb's bike, shish-kebbabbed on the prongs, its rusty rear sparking the floor.

Barb ducked as the forklift smashed through another wall. She grabbed for her gun again. Pryzer wrenched the big machine to the right. The Laser-Chaser fell from Barb's grasp, went flying into the dark.

She could hear his manic yell as he smashed through walls, over piles of steel debris. With a tortured scream of metal, he speared another car, made a quick, shaky turn and burst outside, barreling across the dockyards at a sickening speed. Barb peered ahead, sucked in a breath and stared.

"You crazy bastard – stop!"

If Pryzer saw it he didn't care. The concrete wall loomed up ahead. The prongs struck it head on, and the forklift came to a bone-jarring halt.

Barb held tight. The impact rattled her teeth, took her breath away. She struggled to her feet, ignoring the brand-new bruises, leaped up on the bike's seat. Grabbing a twisted length of bumper off the skewered car, she hefted it to her shoulder and went after Pryzer.

Pryzer's hands appeared, gripping the edge of the control cabin. He pulled himself erect, stared at her and grinned. He had one black eye; blood trickled down his cheek.

"Well, if this isn't something, now. If I was of a sensitive nature, I'd be real touched. Barb Wire's last stand. Desperate and alone, the lovely maiden stood her ground . . ."

"You keep talking, I'm going to throw up," Barb said.

She whipped the metal weapon up from her side, brought it down hard. Pryzer jerked his hands off the railing. He looked at her, counted his fingers and grinned, reached down and brought up his pistol and aimed it at her head.

"I try not to get all emotional about my work, but vaporizin' your springy ass is going to feel so fine . . ."

He made a big show of closing one eye, peering down the barrel, like he had to be sure and not miss her from two feet away.

"Bye, bye, Barb. It's sure been fun."

"Bye," Barb said. She gave him a saucy wink. "You mind a little free advice, hon?"

"Huh?" Pryzer looked confused. "What're you talking about?"

"Don't worry so much about what's in front of you. Think about what's sneaking up *behind* . . ."

Pryzer laughed. "Isn't anything snea – WAAAH!"

The big hook snared the side of the forklift, wrenched it off the ground. Pryzer turned white. The gun dropped from his hand and he reached out frantically, clawing for a hold as the big machine twisted in the air.

Pryzer's scream cut through the night. Barb held on, straddling one of the forklift's prongs. Looking up, she saw the heavy cable rising into the sky, saw the giant steel crane above that. The small control cabin was lost in the darkness, but she didn't have to guess who was there.

The crane whined with power, and the forklift rose higher and higher off the ground, turning in slow and lazy circles in the air. The bikes and the derelict car slipped a foot down the prongs, slipped again and held. The massive machine swayed, the cable gave an agonizing groan.

Okay, Axel, let's not push it . . . get me the hell down from here . . .

Pryzer scrambled free of the cabin, making his way to the roof of the forklift's cab, cursing under his breath. Barb grabbed a handhold and followed. Just this once, she agreed with Pryzer one hundred percent. Getting as far away from the hanging mass as she could seemed a hell of a good idea.

He glanced down, saw her, kicked out with one foot. Barb ducked, caught herself as she started to slide down the slanting metal roof.

"Stay where you are," Pryzer warned her, "get away form me!"

"I'll bet you didn't like to share as a kid," Barb said. "I'll bet you wanted all the toys for yourself."

Pryzer glared. He was holding tight with both hands. Blood stung his eyes, but he wouldn't let go to wipe it out.

"What I'm thinking," Barb said, "you've got a thing about heights. I expect you get dizzy, you look out and see things *way* down there, am I right? Everything swaying back and forth, everything so *far* down . . ."

"Shut up. I'm in the military service, you dumb bitch. We're trained for this. We go high all the time."

"Not *this* high, I bet. This is *really* high, Colonel."

Barb pulled herself on to the bottom of the giant hook.

"What – what the hell are you doing?" Pryzer stared at her. "Get away from there!"

Barb hung on with both hands, stood, and pumped her legs. The massive load was already swinging in a slow arc, and Barb's motion gave it an extra push.

"You ever have a swing when you were a kid? Or you just sit around pulling the wings off bugs?"

"Stop that, *stop it*!" Pryzer kicked out wildly, trying to reach her with his feet.

Barb showed him a wicked grin. "I wonder how

much we can get it swinging? I mean, before the son of a bitch snaps? If you were to come up here and help . . ."

Pryzer yelled in fury and came at her, stalking across the slanting roof. Barb kicked out, him in the belly and drove him back. The hanging mass gave a precarious lurch. Pryzer looked horrified. He stopped, spread his legs for traction, caught his breath and came at Barb again. Barb lashed out with her foot. Pryzer jerked back, grabbed her leg – drew himself toward her. Held her and slapped her hard across the cheek.

Barb cried out, tried to back away. Pryzer hit her again. Barb took the blow, slammed herself against him and thrust a knee at his crotch.

Pryzer felt it coming, blocked the blow with his wounded thigh. He backed off, face twisted in pain. Barb took advantage of the moment and came at him. He rolled aside, held her wrist in a painful lock and threw her over the edge.

Barb opened her mouth to cry out. The scream stuck in her throat. There was nothing below but darkness, the ground yawning up far below. She reached out blindly, found the side of the roof with one hand, held on, ground her teeth together. Her hand slipped, nearly slid free. She yelled out in anger and desperation, threw her other hand up, found the edge with her fingertips, held on tight. Gathering all her strength, she forced herself back on top.

Pryzer laughed, held on to his perch and lashed out with one foot to kick her off again. Barb grabbed his boot, twisted hard. Pryzer shouted and slammed down on his back.

Barb crawled past him, scrambling for the derrick's big hook. She saw it, then, saw the red lever on the cable, just above the hook. She leaped for it, grabbed the cable with one hand. Pryzer came after her, clutched at her legs. She kicked out, jabbed at his face with her heel, tearing at his flesh.

Pryzer laughed, shaking his head to sling the blood away. "I've never – felt so close to you, Barb. I think I feel romance in the air!" He howled at his joke. "It's – just like my favorite song. I got – you, babe . . ."

Barb bent her knees, kicked out and broke free, buried her boot in his mouth.

"*Huuuh!*" Pryzer blinked, spat blood and teeth, reached for her again. Barb shook him off, grabbed for the hook and swung herself high. She looked down at Pryzer, grasped the red lever and pulled it as hard as she could . . .

The hook let go.

The massive forklift dropped free and plunged dizzily toward the ground, toward the darkness ten stories below. Pryzer stood on the roof of the cab, looking up at Barb, looking slightly puzzled, looking like he wondered just what would happen next, why he was going down and Barb was going up. Something, he decided, must be screwed up somewhere . . .

One second . . . two . . .

Thunder shook the earth. A fireball blossomed, the heat so intense Barb felt it high above.

She hung on tight. Looked down below and shook her head.

"Don't call me *babe*, man. Don't *ever* do that . . ."

260

Thirty-four

The plane was an old Swedish 700, pre-war. It seemed to strain on its leash as the pilot juggled the jets, hoping for a semblance of the sweet song they sang when she was new. The airfield was surrounded by a high, chain-link fence topped with killer wire. Sandbags were stacked at the only entry gate. A full platoon of U.N. troopers watched everyone who even came near.

Corrina was certain they were all watching her – that every man there was waiting for her to snap, go berserk and charge the gate, an automatic weapon clutched in each hand, determined to get on the plane and take her vital information to Canada and the world . . .

She had to laugh at herself. Maybe there'd be some dramatic background music as well. A pathetic surge, a swelling of violins. Or maybe they'd carry her off in a green body bag. That seemed a more likely final scene. A bullet through the head, a beautiful speech with her last gasping breath, her eyes softly close . . .

"Shit," Corrina said aloud.

"What's that?" Willis raised a brow.

"I said, *shit*. You ever heard the word before?"

"Well, yeah. As a matter of fact I have . . ." He saw the anguish, the anger in her eyes.

"He's going to be here," he said. "I've got a real good feeling about this."

"Oh, fine."

If he'd stayed here . . . if he hadn't gone back for Barb . . .

She tried to toss the thought aside, tell herself she ought to be ashamed of herself, but she couldn't bring it off. The woman Axel had gone back for was the same woman who'd saved their hides – *and* sold them down the river at the same time. What the hell was she supposed to think of Barb Wire?

Beside her, Willis drew in a breath. She looked past him at the plane and felt her heart swell up in her throat. The whine of the jets was rising, the plane was moving sluggishly forward, jockeying into the wind. She watched as the last few passengers hurried aboard.

"Oh, God!" Corrina clutched at the chain-link fence, pressed her face against the wire. "Damn it, you can't leave me here . . ."

"Take it easy," Willis said. "We'll, uh – do something, okay?"

"What? What the hell do you have in mind?"

"We could blast our way through. Overpower them somehow. I've had police training, you know."

Corrina shook he head. "I already went through that scenario. We don't make it. We all get killed."

"All of us?"

"Every last one."

"Sounds reasonable." Willis said. "On the other hand, maybe we could –"

Willis stopped. Corrina stared past him, grabbed his arm. He turned, then, saw them running down the narrow road out of the dark, past the high derricks, past the black harbor.

"Axel, Christ, I thought you were dead!"

"Yeah. So did I." He glanced at the plane and shook his head. "You ever see one of these mothers take off on time? *This* one takes off on time. How do you figure that?"

"We were just discussing the possibilities of a suicidal charge," Willis said. "Something quite heroic, fatal and dumb."

Corrina looked at Barb, quickly looked away. "What did you hurry for, Axel? All I can do is stand here and wave. I can't get *on* the thing? I can't even –"

"Don't get excited," Barb said, "no one's missing the goddamn plane."

Corrina glared. "I believed you once. I don't intend to make the same mistake twice."

"You want to live longer, you've got to learn to relax." Barb wiped a hand across her face, looked at her dirty palm in disgust. "That's what I do, and I'm the picture of health."

She turned away from them, then, out of the wind, bent her head slightly. She touched both her eyes with her fingertips, turned back to Corrina Devonshire.

Corrina gasped in disbelief, brought a hand to her mouth. "Oh, God. You – you've got them. You didn't –"

"No, I didn't. You trust a crown like Big Fatso, you deserve to lose your ass. I'd kinda like to hold on to mine."

Corrina laid a hand lightly on her arm. "I'm – I'm sorry. I was wrong about you, Barb. Terribly wrong."

"Story of my life. Get on that plane and save the world. We'll call it even."

Willis rolled his eyes in wonder, left them and ran toward the entryway.

"All right, hold that plane. I'm Chief Willis, Steel Harbor Police. This is official business, men."

Axel shielded Corrina while she popped the lenses into her eyes. Corrina blinked, her eyes suddenly turning a startling cobalt blue.

"Barb —"

"Shut up. Get on the plane."

Corrina tried to speak, finally kissed Barb lightly on the cheek, and ran for the entryway. Willis and a stern-looking sergeant were waiting. Corrina stepped through the gate, stood perfectly still before the retinal scanner.

"Ret-in-al scan veri-fied . . . citi-zen is approved by all governments concerned . . ."

Corrina let out a breath, smiled at Willis and walked rapidly across the runway toward the waiting plane. Halfway there she stopped, turned and looked back at Axel and Barb . . .

Axel held her close. He brushed a strand of hair out of her eyes.

"You're not quite as neutral as everybody thinks, Barb. A lot of people are going to be disappointed to hear that."

"Keep it between us. Don't go blabbing it to everyone." She looked into his eyes. "Why did you do it, Axel? Why did you come back for me?"

"I couldn't leave you twice. I — damn it, Barb, there was a lot between us. You know that and so do I."

"There still is. Do I have to tell you that?"

"No, you don't have to tell me a thing." Axel looked past her. "Corrina's on the plane. She's home free. That was my job and now it's done."

"No. No, it's not." Barb pushed him gently away.

"Get her there. She needs you. Do what has to be done. After that . . ."

"After that I'll be back. For good this time. I promise, Barb –"

"No." She pressed a finger to her lips. "No, don't promise, Axel. Just say it, okay?"

"It doesn't end like that again, Barb."

"Good. I'll keep that in mind. Now get out of here."

He held her, kissed her hard, turned toward the entry gate. She watched him pause at the retinal scanner, then run across the concrete to join Corrina.

"My, are those real tears I see? Amazing. Absolutely amazing."

"Shut up, Willis."

"Let's see . . ." Willis closed one eye in thought. "You gave up all that dough, gave up the lenses as well, let your true love walk out of your life *again* – for a good cause, no less. My God, all this in one day, too. Is this a good streak in you I simply don't know about?"

"Don't make too much out of it. I don't want to start a lot of talk."

"Well, still . . ."

Without looking at him, she reached into the vee of her shirt, let him take a peek at a gold debit card, dropped it back in place.

"Big Fatso won't need his seven-hundred-fifty thou. Might as well go to a worthy cause."

"Like the Barb Wire Foundation, right?" Willis grinned. "Where do you go from here? As a former city official with some knowledge of both the local and military situation, I do not recommend Steel Harbor."

265

"I hear Paris is nice this time of year."

"Paris is nice any time of year."

"Yeah. I heard that too."

She looked past him to the airfield, watched the plane scream down the runway, watched it roar overhead with a noise that shook the ground. She stood there and watched it until the winking lights disappeared.

Willis looked at her. "I guess I'd be out of line if I asked if you, ah – thought about including any company in your travel plans . . ."

Barb gave him a friendly peck on the cheek. "I guess not, but thanks for asking anyway. Goodbye, Willis."

Willis sighed. "I *hate* these sudden attacks of romance. I feel like I'm falling in love. God, that's annoying . . ."

"Happens all the time," Barb said. "Get in line, pal."

War creates fiction and fact. The winners write the histories; the losers write the legends and the myths. *Who were the heroes and who were the villains?* one may ask. The statues and the paintings in museums seldom tell the whole story of a monumental event.

Of the many prominent names that emerged from the Second American Civil War, that of Dr. Corrina Devonshire must find a place somewhere near the top of the list. Dr. Devonshire lived. She was real. Though many of the adventures attributed to her were, one imagines, exaggerated or totally untrue.

Two of the people usually associated with the Corrina Devonshire tales are Axel Hood and Barbara Kopetski – popularly known as Barb Wire. These two people may very well have existed. If they did, however, we have no clear record of them now. And, truly, it is not the names that matter, for the men and women they represent are very real. If we have lost their names, we have not lost the truth of their deeds. That is something we can never forget.

– Johnny Gray Wolf, PhD, *Fall From Glory* (2032),
University of the New Sioux Nation Press.